W

A

N

WAN

A NOVEL

DAWN PROMISLOW

Freehand Books acknowledges the financial support for its publishing program provided by the Canada Council for the Arts and the Alberta Media Fund, and by the Government of Canada through the Canada Book Fund.

Canada Council   Conseil des Arts   Alberta   Canada
for the Arts   du Canada   Government

Freehand Books
515 – 815 1st Street sw   Calgary, Alberta   T2P 1N3
www.freehand-books.com

Book orders: UTP Distribution
5201 Dufferin Street   Toronto, Ontario   M3H 5T8
Telephone: 1-800-565-9523   Fax: 1-800-221-9985
utpbooks@utpress.utoronto.ca   utpdistribution.com

Library and Archives Canada Cataloguing in Publication
Title: Wan / Dawn Promislow.
Names: Promislow, Dawn, author.
Identifiers: Canadiana (print) 20210368608 | Canadiana (ebook) 20210368616 | ISBN 9781988298993 (softcover) | ISBN 9781990601002 (EPUB) | ISBN 9781990601019 (PDF)
Classification: LCC PS8631.R64 W36 2022 | DDC C813/.6 —DC23

Edited by Deborah Willis
Book design by Natalie Olsen
Cover image © kkgas/Stocksy.com
Author photo by Eli Amon
Printed on FSC® certified paper and bound in Canada by Marquis

MIX
Paper from
responsible sources
FSC   FSC® C103567
www.fsc.org

TO MY PARENTS

A JOURNALIST CAME to interview me once in my studio on Columbus Avenue. She arrived at the door, a young, breathless woman, her coat on for the snow, her black wool hat, her boots: it was a winter day. I knew right away it was a mistake, I shouldn't have invited her to my studio, my space. The space felt suddenly small and crowded, the two of us standing there, I felt I would not breathe, that I must ask us to leave. But I was polite, I held myself. What choice did I have?

She sat for an hour on the wooden chair, I on the other. My studio had no view, but I needed no view. The tall sashed window overlooked the alleyway between two buildings, and the black fire stairwell. The room was filled on the wooden floor, against the walls, with my canvases, and frames, wooden ones, stacked in a corner, shelves and shelves of paints and jars of turpentine. And my easel, one easel only, in the one corner, where it had the light that I felt was enough. Enough. Only enough.

It was a room without features.

The journalist asked me questions about my painting: the one, the one that was my breakthrough, the one you ask about. She asked about my process. She asked about South Africa.

About my process I could speak. About South Africa I could not. And then I said, should we have a coffee downstairs? The coffee shop is a few doors down. Perhaps she felt relieved, she said then, yes, yes, certainly Ms. Kline. It's Jacqueline, please, I said. But it was too late. There was no possibility of intimacy. And wasn't it always like this, with me?

We went down the elevator together, walked the few doors to the coffee shop, I was not wearing my boots, only my shoes, I remember that. I had in mind to return as soon as possible to the studio, to my solitude there. The young man who'd been working in the coffee shop many months — more months than he'd planned — greeted me, he knew me. Or should I say: he knew my coffee habits. What time I came in (ten a.m., and then again, at noon). What I ordered (a small filtered coffee). Where I sat (at the small table next to the window). That's what he knew. And he knew how I paid (debit card).

The journalist and I drank coffee (she, tea, I remember), we sat at my usual table, and I watched the steamed-up windows, snow flaking outside. I can't remember what we spoke about, we limped around subjects: what I was working on now, how I liked New York, did I travel much? (I did not.) Perhaps we spoke about some current exhibitions. But it ended, at last. Her coat, her black hat, her boots, I watched her, her young figure, walk down the street under the soft, falling snow, towards the subway.

A few days later her article appeared. She'd taken a photo of me, it was black-and-white, I felt it didn't reveal much. My figure, my slight figure, on that wooden chair, a blank wall behind me, my face, and my dark hair curved on one shoulder.

Howard was amused, he brought the newspaper into our bedroom where I still lay that morning. It's alright, he said. I remember sitting up and reading it, I had to turn the lamp on to read it, in my dim room.

The article was alright. It didn't say much. She'd written about process, some technical things. She mentioned the usual: the clarity, the light, the simplicity, of my work. But where did that clarity, that light, that simplicity come from? She had asked, but I had been unable to say, I have always been unable to say, until now. Until now.

For a moment I felt annoyed with the journalist. She wasn't very good at her job, I thought. She was too young, she lacked knowledge of deep things, she lacked knowledge of South Africa. But then I thought, it is I who is wrong, too. These interviews are no good; they are useless. They are even deceptive. I suddenly felt like a liar. But I wasn't a liar; not really. Not really a liar.

Howard said then: it's the editor's fault. They send people who don't know about some other country's history. And then: ah, whatever.

It's really alright though, the article's alright, he said. It was.

But I never invited a journalist to my studio again.

And then: an image of my mother came to me. My mother, long gone, buried in the dusty cemetery near Villiers. If my mother had seen and read the article, she would have said:

a lovely picture of you, Jacqueline. Lovely! And I thought: what had that to do with anything? The familiar twinge of irritation, I felt it, as I imagined her faint voice across that black phone line, I almost heard it.

PERHAPS WHEN one is old one feels that each word must be the truth.

I'm too old to hold on to this story any more. So I'm going to tell it to you. That's all. I will tell it. I never told that journalist, and I've never told anyone at all. I've never told it.

I STARTED MY PAINTING in 1972. I had a studio where I painted at the end of my garden, in the northern suburbs of Johannesburg.

I'd been painting for years. I was thirty-two.

In 1972 we also hired a new maid. We hired her, a Black maid, she joined Emily to help with the house and children. Josias, looking after the garden, had been with us for a while. So there we were: I, Howard, the two children, and the three domestic workers, who had rooms off the stone yard at the back of the house.

After my coffee and grapefruit, which I had on the patio, and a brief glance through the newspaper, I would go down into my studio. The children were at school, Howard at work, so I had, in the mornings, peace and solitude. You, you would know how I loved that. My studio was invisible from the house, it was hidden and shaded by the deepest trees, you could hear them rustle, like beings. A stone step. A push on the wooden door. A musty smell. And I was in. My canvases stacked against the whitewashed walls. Some light coming through the two windows, but not too much light. It was quite dim. Wooden frames of many sizes, how many possibilities these held! I would settle at once.

Sometimes I would hear one of the dogs barking, but that's all.

In the afternoons the children came home, and my peace was done. I was usually in my room resting by the time they were home. And then later I would go out onto the lawn, lie on my pool-chair, and watch them swim. How happy, how carefree they were. Their bright bathing suits flashed, and the sun glinted on the water, its blueness and white crests in the children's wake. Otherwise the afternoons were still, sometimes the dogs came down and barked at the splashing, and once Chester our white Labrador jumped into the water too. He never did it again after that, but it remained a vivid image in all of our minds I think, the day and the moment Chester went swimming.

Helena said to me last month, remember when Chester went swimming? She laughed. We were sitting in my living room, soft light, a winter night. Why did he never go swimming again after that, she said. Perhaps he didn't like it, I said, after he'd tried it. Poor Chester, Helena said then. Why did she think of Chester that evening, that quiet evening in New York?

LATER, those afternoons at the pool, the children lay on the stones alongside and talked, or argued with each other, about this or that. I'd have to intervene, stop fighting, I'd say, stop! Then they'd run off, to the end of the garden, into their tree-house, hidden by other, taller trees, and shrubs. I'd hear them talking softly then, playing their pretend games I suppose. I'd read. My book, any book that I had with me. It would have been fiction, in those days I read mostly fiction. Nadine Gordimer's new story collection was out, I had a hardcover copy. I would lend it to my mother after, I thought. I pictured her: on her red-polished porch, overlooking her garden, dry in the Free State sun, a buzz of cicadas by.

But my painting. I struggled with it. How many canvases I tried, then discarded — tried, then discarded. I spent weeks on one canvas, each day I came to it, and moved something in it, I moved a line, or a shadow. I mixed a new shade of colour, my colours that I loved so much. Each day the colours looked a little different, yet the same. My brush, so firm in my hand, like my hand itself. The light in the room would change, so slowly, as the morning wore on. The shades deepened, then lightened. Did I need more light? But I didn't need more light, I knew that. The light in my room, my studio, had a dimness which I loved.

The struggle with that painting had been going on for months, I don't know how many months, but many. I felt the struggle to be a part of me. I'd sit in the studio on the wooden chair I had, a hard chair, but deep and low. I'd found it in a neighbour's garage once, and asked him for it. I'd sit, and shut my eyes. I had an idea that if I shut my eyes the image of the painting would be clearer to me, as it had been all night, in my dreams. Perhaps it was.

At last I'd emerge for lunch. Out of the trees, into the sunlight, although the trees were always close and rustling. I loved them, too.

I would sit on the patio then, Emily would bring me lunch, she knew exactly what to bring, because it was always the same. Sliced avocado, a cut tomato; lemon. And my tea. A silence hung in the afternoon.

I would think of the hanging afternoon, so hot, where my mother would be, sitting on her porch. Her husband — my father — at his shop. She alone, but for Maggie, sitting on a chair under the eave in the yard at the back. Flies, many flies. Maggie's pale blue uniform and white apron, her scarf, her *doek*, a little crooked on her head. I'd call my mother later, I thought.

I had nothing to tell her, perhaps I could think of something about the children, because her first question always, how are the children. Perhaps that was her only question.

OUR NEW MAID fit in soon enough, Emily showed her everything. Josias carried on in his inscrutable way, he played his radio in the afternoons in his room, I'd hear it if I stepped out into their yard. And then he would be cleaning the pool later, when the children were done swimming. I'd come out again with my tea then and sit on the patio, in the afternoon sun. But still shaded. I'd watch Josias's rhythmic movements with the pool net, he was like a shadow, and so lean he was. The pool so still: pale blue, and deep.

Twice a week I drove Helena to her ballet class. Her pale-pink attire: tights, leotard, ballet shoes. Her hair pulled back into a ponytail, Emily would help her with that: brushing, brushing, smoothing, smoothing the hair.

Sometimes I'd go into the ballet class and watch, sitting on a chair to the side. Helena was eight, then.

Other times, during her lesson, I'd drive to my paint shop, the art shop. I'd spend an hour browsing the paints and canvases, the tubes and bottles and brushes, the rows and rows on the wooden shelves. Eric, who managed the shop, was a young man, he knew me well. I had been going there for years, and he'd been there since he finished art college. He was building his own portfolio, hoping for gallery representation one day. They were visits of love for me, to that shop. Sometimes I'd try new oils, a new brand, but not often. I was so particular. I was so bound by habit, and Eric often laughed with me about that. No one is as particular as you, he'd say. Why don't you try a new pigment, a new brush? No, no, I cannot do that, I'd say. It was true, it really was true.

And then I'd pick Helena up again, her flushed face, her hair falling in strands from its ponytail. She was a serious child, she didn't laugh much, perhaps she resembled me, I think that might be true.

Stephen was eleven. He loved to swim, there were those afternoons in the pool, hours and hours: he splashing, jumping, then lying down alongside in the sun, then jumping or diving in again. He'd swim lengths as he got older, like his father. His father who'd been a champion swimmer, in his day.

And then in the evenings, close to seven but still light, Howard came home. How long it took me to get used to the failing light here, when the late afternoon comes! You who've always lived here might not feel the difference, but I — I feel it, every time.

Howard still had so much energy when he came home. There'd be tumult when he arrived, Josias first opening the garage door for his car, I could hear the door grind open, or perhaps I just imagine I could hear it, from my bedroom where I'd be. The dogs, then, barking. Laughter from the kitchen and the maids, how Howard made them laugh! The children: Dad, Dad, you know what happened today? Dad! Dad! And then Howard would get to our room, hello, hello. He'd look at me searchingly, hi sweetheart. Perhaps I was beautiful, then.

Howard would change out of his suit — hardly rumpled — his briefcase already abandoned in his study across the hall. We'd head to the dining room for dinner.

Emily served dinner. Josias helped in the kitchen, scurrying in or out with a pot, a heavier one, or fetching a serving spoon, something forgotten by Emily, or washing the pots, after. Emily was a good cook, better than me. Perhaps her previous employer had taught her, I think that might be true. The children were raucous, talkative, at dinner, Helena quieter, but also competing in her voice with her day's stories. I think I was quiet, I probably ate quietly, I feel that is true. Perhaps I was firm with the children, reprimanding them about their table manners: take your elbows off the table, off! Don't talk while you're chewing, don't do that!

AFTER DINNER I'd call my mother. I'd hear her voice, faint across the line. I'd picture the thin black telephone wire that connected us, from Johannesburg where I was, across and between the pale yellow mine dumps, through Vereeniging, Vanderbijlpark, into the Orange Free State, its brown plains and the brown Vaal River snaking, to her, to her black telephone in the dim hallway, her wooden floor. You wouldn't know those black telephones, that's what phones used to look like — dinosaurs — you see them in antique shops now. I pictured my mother's small hands, pale, and her wedding ring, almost as old as her.

I have that ring, here in New York, but I don't wear it. I have an idea my mother would've liked me to wear it, but I cannot wear someone else's ring. This is true, too.

We'd make arrangements on the phone for her and my father's next visit. They'd bring cling peaches, she said, they're just ripening now. I pictured the fruit trees behind her house, many of them, they stood next to the circle washing line, idle in the sun, and near the tall swing with creaking ropes, where I had swung, swung, as a girl, through the years. There were the rocks and stones nearby with cacti planted, and the lizards which lay and baked, and which I'd see startle and disappear, in a moment. A rustle, only.

The peaches will be lovely, I'd say, thank you. I imagined the cardboard crate loaded into the back of their Peugeot, Klaas the driver would have done that, and the crate arriving in our driveway, unloaded then by Josias. A mound of dusky orange fruits, so many. Holding within them the Free State sun, that warm and warming sun. Their round perfection: a Cézanne.

IN 1972 the political situation continued in a terrible stasis. We were deeply aware of our peace, and what it concealed and cost. Nelson Mandela was in prison — it was already ten years — we dared not say his name where we could be heard. We fretted about the disgrace of millions of Black people, disenfranchised, and underfoot.

Then we lived our days on, as before.

THERE WERE THE three domestic workers in our yard. We called them servants. Howard paid them, as well as he could, I assume. Do I know how much he paid them? I do not. I had nothing to do with money. I also had no interest in money. I bought the maids their uniforms, Emily gained weight every year and needed a new one, almost every year. She and I laughed about that, it was a minor inconvenience to me. Once she said, okay ma'am, I will just wear the smaller one, it's just tight, doesn't matter. I said, no, no Emily, I'll buy a new one. And I did. Of course. Why did she gain weight? She liked food I suppose. She was susceptible. She ate a lot of *mieliemeel,* that's what I thought. I bought the three of them their own meat at the butcher, for their stews, it was stewing beef. Stephen loved those stews, he would eat a plate himself at night if Howard and I were out, while he sat with them in the kitchen. How do I know that? Emily told me, she laughed when she told me, and I laughed too. We laughed a lot about small things like that. The truth of it is I loved Emily: her solidity of character; her sense of humour. Her intelligence.

Sometimes I would talk to her about the political situation, it was a conversation of tremendous awkwardness.

It will change one day, I would say. Yes ma'am, I hope so, she'd answer. But she looked doubtful, and I'm sure I looked doubtful, and pained, and there was nothing else I felt able to say.

Once I thought I must say something more. You know . . . I said. Mandela? She looked at me, startled.

He will come out one day you know, I said. And he will lead this country.

I felt anguished as I said it. Emily was still looking at me, I couldn't discern what she felt, what she intended with her look. She nodded. She said nothing.

As the months and years went on I tried to say a version of this every once in a while. It felt necessary. It felt necessary to say it. I felt like a terrible person, as I said it. And then I'd go to my bedroom and feel such rage at our situation, and shame.

JOSIAS SPOKE very little English. He had come only recently to Johannesburg from the Transkei, and he was a young man. I've mentioned the sound of the radio from his room, which I'd hear in the late afternoons. Voices in his language (which was Xhosa), and music. He wore the same tattered shorts every day, they hung on him, as he was so lean, and a loose shirt, dun-coloured. I knew nothing about him. He had a pass to work for us, that's all I knew. On his day off he disappeared through the whitewashed back gate in the morning, dressed in long pants, and he returned in the evening, sometimes I'd see him walking up the street from the main road, where his bus would have been. I pictured a long bus ride, and slow.

Crowded. Through the streets of Johannesburg, to . . . where? To Soweto perhaps, distant and dun, under the wide pale sky, where he might have friends. I don't know, I didn't know.

Stephen once asked me to explain to Maya, his younger daughter, how it was, how it was that I knew so little about Josias and his life. Maya was doing a school project on apartheid-era South Africa, something like that. Stephen suggested going out for tea and chatting, Maya would love that, he said. I pictured us at our favourite coffee shop, the black-and-white iced cookies she liked so much. But then I felt overwhelmed. I thought: where to begin? And where to end? So I told Stephen the girls were better off reading books, the many history books about it, I would not be able to have tea that day. I really said that, I did.

JOSIAS CLEANED the pool every day, sweeping, sweeping with the long pool brush. I had an idea it was a job of peace and calm, but now — now — I think it was me, just me, who felt that. I'd see him fiddling with the filter at the pool's edge, and sometimes he'd have broken conversations with Howard about the chlorine levels; I knew nothing about that. One evening Howard took him in the car to the hardware shop, they must have had a problem, and I imagine them there, the two, talking and puzzling over the pool and its chlorine levels. There was laughing between them. Howard — I've said it before — was a kind man.

Josias fed the dogs their meat, that was another task he had, then he'd sit on his chair, his wooden chair, next to the laundry lines, smoking a cigarette. My mother visiting had once complained that the dogs' bowls were dirty and with flies, she had gone out to the backyard to call Emily.

Your Josias is very lazy you know, she said.

I didn't care, didn't care about things like that. I thought of Josias, as I say, as a peaceful person, and graceful, in his ways. But I am speaking about his temperament, which I could see, I have no idea what went on behind that, in his mind. Whom he loved, who loved him, what he had left behind, in the Transkei. I don't know.

The new maid had told us her name was Tiny. The name struck me right away, she wasn't small. And, like Emily and Josias, she looms large, gigantic, in my mind. Even now.

ONE DAY EARLY that year Howard came home from work and told me he had a problem. We were going to bed, I was reading, my lamp on, and he had come in from his study. He'd been working late.

Jack Benator knows a lawyer who must go underground, Howard said. (Jack was Howard's colleague.) This lawyer's a fine man, he's working for the resistance, Jack wants to help him, Howard said. I felt a stab of pride. Howard, who believed in the resistance, as I did.

The guy needs somewhere to stay, Howard said, for a short while. Until they find him a permanent place. We can fix up the garden room near your studio.

Howard was thinking of an old room, a small stone struc-ture at the end of our garden. It had a tiny bathroom, never used. Perhaps it had been built as a pool change-room at one time, I don't know. We used it only as a storeroom.

What are you talking about, I said. I felt alarmed. It sounded ridiculous. It was, on the face of it, ridiculous. We argued about it for several days, always at night, in our bedroom.

Howard said it wouldn't bother us, we didn't even know the man. We would be kept out of it, he would just be using an old room we had. The security police likely had no idea where this man was, if they even knew about him in the first place.

I thought Howard was going too far, much too far. I became angry with him and he was angry with me.

Howard and I didn't often argue.

Then I thought: that room is hidden, nobody goes there, or anywhere near. I suppose it's alright for a few weeks, it's a small thing, and it's temporary. That's what I remember, what I remember thinking.

And Howard was determined. Someone had asked him to help, and he said he would. That's how Howard was, always was.

I suppose you could say I capitulated.

WE HAD JOSIAS move an old iron bed into the room. I had bedding, sheets and towels, a pillow. A blanket, I put them all there. Josias had cleaned the bathroom with its tub and toilet. I ran the tap to check the water. It came out in spurts, the pipes long unused, but then it flowed smoothly, and I knew it was fine. I put bathroom tissue, some bars of soap, how I remember them, stacked in a small tower on the sill. Howard had remembered an old bar fridge we had in our garage, Josias carried it down in his barrow, I watched him wheel it down to the room, I was watching through my bedroom window. An image that returns and returns: Josias, lean Josias, crookedly wheeling his barrow with the old white fridge atop, down the grass, down the hill, to the trees. And then: invisible. You couldn't see the stone room from the house.

I stood later in the room, to see if everything was in final order. A shaft of sunlight fell across the old floor, dust motes hung, and twirled slowly. A safe place, I thought. We'd also put an old wooden table and chair, there was a light. I had an idea the light wasn't bright enough, it was just a bulb hanging from the whitewashed ceiling. He'd be a reader, I thought, he'd be reading. The weak light? I put it out of mind, I wouldn't worry about it.

Before sweeping the room Josias had moved the stored things out, he'd stacked them in the garage, and some I had him throw out. I told him a friend was coming to stay, and I told Emily and Tiny that too. They may have been puzzled, but they didn't say. Emily and Tiny didn't really care about the garden, what went on there, because their domain was the house, and the yard where their own rooms were.

And the children? The children. I had taken, we had taken, care to teach our children from the beginning that the government, the system, in our country was wrong. They understood, profoundly I think, how much it meant to Howard and me. They surely could see the expression on Howard's face when he spoke about it, could feel my anxiety and anger when I did. Long ago we had told them that one day, if things didn't change, we would leave the country, Dad would move his job to an overseas country, and we would leave. The children knew, also, not to talk about this outside our home, they felt, no doubt, the fear and silence that surrounded us. A man working for the resistance was going to stay in our garden room. They were not to tell anyone, that's all. The grandparents were not to hear about it, no one was to hear about it.

So our house was safe. A safe harbour for a man — for a cause — in need.

Did the man in the garden room haunt the children's dreams later, much later, when they were at school in New York? I don't know. They never said. They spoke of him as 'the man from the resistance,' and moved on to other things. They were strong children. They were not, perhaps, like me.

I'VE MENTIONED the grandparents who weren't to know about the fugitive man, but Helena and Stephen had only one set of grandparents. Howard's mother had died soon after Stephen was born, and his father before that, I had never met him.

His mother had spoken English with an accent, a Russian accent, I remember it. She had a soft voice, sometimes you couldn't hear or detect the accent, and she spoke little. Sometimes I hear, on the streets here, a person with a strong Russian accent, and I remember her, Howard's mother, at once. She had emigrated from Lithuania in 1931, before the war — or should I say, she had escaped from Lithuania, just in time. She was Jewish. Howard's father too.

Howard grew up next to Johannesburg's city centre. He and his parents boarded with another family, they had the second floor, that's all. I never saw it, but Howard told me about it, described it: its bareness, and how cramped it was. There were chickens in a coop at the back, and a narrow laneway. Howard's father worked in a menswear shop, he worked for his landlord. They struggled, they always struggled.

Perhaps my mother-in-law never got over the trauma of leaving her home, her country, and her parents, everyone left behind, and the long years after 1940, when she heard nothing, nothing, from them. No letter. No letters. She'd mention often, even when I knew her — during the short while that I knew her — the letters, the letters, that never came, that never came from Europe, after 1940. From her village, from her *shtetl,* whose name, she told me once, was Rakishok. A silence, a silence from there, no sound or trace of anything, anyone, ever again.

Howard was an only child, like me. We joked, from the beginning, that it's what bound us. Of course, it is not. I think of Howard as the rescued one, the salvaged one, from the wreckage of the war that his parents left behind. I feel that it was enough, full enough, for his parents to have brought one rescued person into the world, brought him into being, and they could not manage another. I do not know, though, if this is true. Perhaps my mother-in-law was physically unable to conceive again, perhaps she had miscarriages, how would I know. She would never have spoken of such a thing: she who spoke so little, to begin with.

I've understood since that my mother-in-law was a person of absences, and erasures. Something I learned about other people among us, too. But that was later; much later.

In any case, I think she and her husband never cared to keep their Jewish traditions, or pass them down, I think it hurt them too much.

And I think Howard felt about it as his parents did. He married me, after all. I, who am a secular Jew.

But here's a thing. Helena travelled to Lithuania a few years ago, in 2009, with her husband. She had always been interested in that history, her grandparents' history.

Howard had only the town's name, Rakishok, to give her. Nothing else. He tried, he tried to remember, but he'd never asked his mother. Helena is interested in absences. I've said it before: she resembles me.

JOSEPH, the lawyer working underground for the resistance, came to our house, to our garden room; in late January. Howard brought him home from work.

It was in the evening, just before dinner.

Joseph, Howard said, as we stood in the lamp-lit hallway. This is my wife, Jacqueline. And Joseph shook my hand.

Thank you, thank you, he said. It won't be for long. I'm so grateful. He was dark-haired and bearded, and thin, he wore silver-rimmed glasses.

He had dinner with us that evening, we spoke nothing of politics or of what he was doing. He was deferential and polite in everything he did, towards the children — he asked them the usual questions about school, about their activities — and towards the servants (of course). The children liked visitors, we didn't have that many, and they boasted about their small achievements: the swim team, the ballet, the A+ grades in school. And then, Howard and I, and he, had a drink in the living room. Or, Howard and I had a drink, he said he didn't drink, he'd have a lime juice and soda, which Emily brought from the kitchen. I barely drank, I don't drink now, and Howard had a glass of wine occasionally, a whisky if he had a guest. We sat, I remember, in the dim, green room — how I loved that room — it was lamp-lit. My living room in New York is a lot like it, perhaps I made it the same. I had some old, small paintings on the walls I had picked up here and there, landscapes mostly, in muted colours. Not my own work.

There were the ochre-coloured and pale-green patterns on the couches, faded. His glasses — Joseph's glasses — flashed a little in the lamplight as he spoke. Howard was more subdued

in his mood than usual, not joking much. I smiled at our guest.
Our guest?

You'll be fine, I said. The room is quite safe, no one knows
it's there, at the end of the garden, under the trees.

He told us he wouldn't come into the house again, and
thank you, thank you, many times, he said.

HOWARD TOOK a flashlight and called Josias, and we walked,
the four of us, down to the room, through the dark garden.
The light pooled and wavered in front of us. We were silent. I'd
never been down to the end of our garden at night. I thought,
then, of its dark beauty and stillness, its breath held. Joseph
carried one small suitcase. I thought to myself, what circum-
stances for this man. Howard continued quieter than usual,
no doubt he felt as I did. What Josias thought, I have no idea.

Please, don't trouble yourselves with the meals, he said.
If you bring me bread, something, once a day, I'll be fine. My
comrades will bring food at night when they come. They can
come through the back gate, the backyard? The servants know
that? I'll tell them, I said. I had a feeling of unease.

But . . . the dogs, I said. What about the dogs? Josias kept
the dogs locked in the yard at night. They weren't watchdogs:
they barked at night if they heard people on the street, but
not much. They were friendly. Chester especially, the Labrador,
was friendly. I'll bring the dogs down tomorrow morning, I
said. To introduce you. I laughed then, and Joseph laughed too.
Josias, I remember, nodded, he thought that was a good idea.

And so it began. What began? Impossible to say simply
what began, but I'll try.

THE NEXT DAY I told Emily to take Joseph a plate of bread and butter, jam, and cheese every morning. I helped Emily prepare the tray, that first time. I told her it must be enough for breakfast and lunch. I told her to add whatever else she wanted. A hard-boiled egg, any leftovers. A bottle of milk. I would add an extra bottle of milk from now on, to our order. Later I had Emily take down an old kettle for his room, and I bought him tea, and then I said to Emily, you know, just take him leftovers from dinner too. I worried. Did he have enough to eat?

I took the dogs later that morning, called them, and they bounded down the grass behind me. I knocked on Joseph's door. The dogs wagged their tails in their usual way, friendly dogs I've said before, Joseph stood on the stone step at his door, how I remember that. He patted them, and laughed. I laughed too. Chester and Teddy, I said. And I felt some relief then, as I said goodbye, have a good day, Joseph, and I walked back up the hill, the dogs having lost interest in Joseph, in me, already, gone off to look for other things in the trees, under the trees.

It became routine: Emily walked down to the garden room twice a day, in the morning, and in the evening. I'd see her in the evening from my bedroom window, walking carefully down the grass, her blue uniform against the green, and her white cap, carrying her tray. Emily's plump figure, that I knew so well. And then, she'd come back up the hill, carrying the white dishes, the dishes he'd used that day.

IT WAS, as I thought about it, absurd. How had this happened, how had we been brought into this situation?

Howard never saw Joseph, he'd just ask me, in the evenings, if everything was alright with him. Yes, yes, fine, I said. Emily takes him food, that's all. I don't see him.

I didn't see him, it's true.

There's nothing to worry about, Howard said. It's got nothing to do with us. Howard had said that many times. It was only partly true, of course. I said nothing.

I FORCED MYSELF to put Joseph and the garden room out of mind, and to continue with my own work. My painting, above all. I had progressed, I felt I was making headway.

It began, the process of my painting, in my bedroom. After lunch I'd go to lie down. My room had a particular light, it faced south, it had the most light in the house. It faced the garden (but you know that, I've told you how I'd watch things in the garden from my window). It was a white room, no colour, apart from a cover on our bed, which was blue. My mother had made the cover, it had many shades of blue. Starting with indigo, a royal blue, it became more pale, in gradations: a dusky navy, then a robin's-egg blue, and finally, a baby blue, very pale. It was made of many patches, it was a patchwork of knitted squares. My mother spent many hours making that cover, she'd made one for each of the children, too. I'm not sure what happened to mine, I don't have it any more. It lay on the end of our bed.

I would think of my mother sitting on her shaded porch, a patch held in her practiced way, her knitting needles, her bag with the tortoiseshell handle alongside her, on a still afternoon. Cicadas. Her miniature cacti on metal stands, many-shaped and many-spiked, small, so small, like creatures, behind her, against the windows of her house.

IN MY BEDROOM I had a rocking chair, its seat was covered in faded blue — so the room was not entirely white, I'm wrong! The chair was old, I had found it in an antique shop, a shop on Oxford Road I went into from time to time.

And then there was my dressing table. It was in the bay

window, the window looking onto the garden. The table was large and a faded ivory, I can't remember where I had found it, perhaps the same shop on Oxford Road. It had its three mirrors, the two on the sides could be moved to change the angle. I would see my profile if I moved the one side. Its surface had on it my hairbrush and comb, my comb was of tortoiseshell, perhaps it had been my mother's. The table had a matching chair. Ivory, an old yellow tinge to it, and a worn, embroidered cushion.

There were also small drawers in the dressing table, where I kept things. Notes I'd written on scraps of paper, and small stones, some from our garden. I had a coloured stone, deep blue, from some other shop. I felt the stone carried within it the sea, or an idea of the sea. The sea was very far away from there, from Johannesburg.

I didn't care for necklaces and bracelets. Howard knew soon after he met me I didn't care for shiny things, for jewellery. Once, for a birthday, he bought me a gold bracelet, of course in South Africa gold was . . . everywhere, and the best gold. The best gold? I don't know if there is such a thing. I still don't know. In any case, I didn't care for it.

I HAD PICTURED HOWARD going at lunchtime during his work day, a short walk down Rissik Street, I knew that jeweller. A busy street, shadowed by old buildings, gloomy in my mind, Black workers lounging around stone doorways on their breaks. The shop was on a corner, its windows were small, just gold lettering with the owner's name, you had to press a buzzer to get in. An old man owned that shop, I heard he passed it down to his son when he died years after. The glass cases, framed with heavy wood, were filled with things of many shapes, larger, and smaller. They glinted, gold. So much gold. And there were diamonds. I cared even less for diamonds. To look into the face of a diamond made me afraid. I don't know why this is, but it's true. It's even true now. I never had a diamond.

The bracelet Howard bought disturbed me right away. I asked — then I begged — Howard to take the bracelet back, to return it to the shop. I felt some distress, Howard could see it in my face. At first he was hurt. Then he was puzzled. Then, he understood. Or, he accepted, he accepted I just didn't want it. Howard understood me.

He took the bracelet back. My wrists were bare. They still are.

BUT: MY BEDROOM. After lunch I would rest in my room. I would lie on my bed, the blue cover at my feet. There was the ceiling, so white, and a shaft of sunlight that moved, so slowly, across. So quiet. No sound at all. The children still at school, the maids taking their break, in their yard. Josias, I would picture him, on his chair with a cigarette — the dogs, alongside, sleeping. Flies in the yard, I imagined them. The grey stones, there. Pale weeds.

I said once I'd buy seeds to grow carrots, or lettuce, did Josias want to plant seeds in his yard? Josias didn't want to do that, Josias didn't do that, even after I brought a packet of seeds home from the hardware store. Josias, Josias, who tended our garden.

But I would lie in my room, the stillness of the afternoon

around me. I would close my eyes. If I lay, and kept still for long enough, the vision would come to me. I thought of it as a spell. Or an honoured, a greatly honoured, guest.

I felt the white room beyond my closed eyes, but it was also within me, illumined by the wide window. And the painting would be there, in my mind.

A large, a very large painting. A rectangle. Lit from within. But by what? It was all white. But not all white, of course not all white. It had many shades and gradations of white, so many I couldn't count or discern them. Ivories, ivories. Glistenings of pallor, so faint. But ordered, into a great harmony. The peace of it, of the painting, would enter me. You might say, into my stream — like a drug. (I've never taken a drug.)

I might fall asleep, then, for a short while. And, now, I picture myself on that bed, recumbent as an effigy, like those figures you know in all the galleries and churches, from long ago. And marble. But I was alive, alive, of course I was alive. I was never a Christian, where did that come from?

MY REST WOULD END with the children coming home, Mom, Mom, they'd call, and then it was the afternoon at the pool, filled with their joy and shrieks, the dogs barking and barking, with them.

I've told you about my mornings, when I'd go down to my studio. Across the grass, past the pool, down the small hill, through the trees, and then . . . my own, my very own, stone room. The worn step, a creak of my door: and in. I'd put on my shirt, I had a shirt on a hook, spattered with years and years of old paint and smelling of turpentine and oil. I'd button it up as I looked around — the familiar dust motes, the familiar dimness. The space, it was enough space. Mine. And then: my canvas. It always surprised me when I found it, it always looked different to how I'd imagined it, in my dreams. Something different in its shading, some brightness missing, or perhaps some new illumination within it; some line subtly moved. I don't know. Sometimes this enraged me. I'd sit on my chair then and think for a while, think about what I should do, what I must do. And then I'd try again. Again.

I would spend weeks on one canvas like that, until I discarded it in disappointment, in despair. I'd take it off the easel and put it to the wall, away from me. And then I'd start again on another. I'd try again. And I'd make a plan in my mind to visit Eric at the art shop, to find a new set of colours, of shades. Perhaps I'd tell Eric my problem.

ONE DAY I drove to Eric and the art store during Helena's ballet class. It wasn't far, it was on a nondescript street, next to some other shops — the Greek grocer, some others. This time I must have looked different, perhaps agitated, because Eric said, are you alright? Ah, yes, no, not really, I said. I laughed. I'm having such trouble, Eric, I said. Such trouble. I shook my head. Your painting? he said. Yes, yes. My painting, I said. Perhaps I'll try something different. Eric laughed then. Ah, don't believe you! he said. I know you.

He did, he did know me. What if I changed my brush, I said. Perhaps a finer one, a smaller one. He went, we went to the back, he showed me some brushes, some others. Eric was patient, he was good at his work. He looked at me searchingly, then. I think you'll figure it out, he said. You will. Of course, in the end, he was right. He was right.

I went into the Greek grocer on my way home, on my way back to the ballet studio. There was an old woman there, I liked talking to her, her English was strongly accented, a little broken. She wore dark dresses — she was an old Mediterranean woman. Her husband would be there too, more idle, he'd be reading a newspaper in his language, its inscrutable alphabet. I mean, inscrutable to me. The shop had fruit and vegetables, I'd get apples and green peppers, and once I bought a crate of tomatoes, I don't know what possessed me. Why so many, ma'am, Emily said when I brought them home. (Josias staggered in with the crate from the car.) Emily and I laughed about that long after, about the day I brought so many tomatoes home. I didn't even know what to cook with them — so many — really. Finally I said to Emily, just put them in a stew, a big stew, every day, but in your stews especially (I meant, the servants' stews) — and she did. I think she liked what she did with her stews for weeks after, I have an idea they were very good. But food didn't concern me much, then.

I DESCRIBE THE peace of my days, but around us, distant from us, was no peace. What went on at night, for instance, in our backyard? Sometimes I'd be woken in the dark night hours, our house so still, by dogs barking. Our dogs? The neighbours' dogs? I couldn't tell. I'd lie then, listening. I thought I heard music, distant rhythmic music, from Josias's room — but perhaps I imagined it. Occasionally there'd be a shout, even a scream, but I couldn't be certain I hadn't simply dreamed it. Perhaps my dreams and sleep were unquiet, that may be true.

And what of Howard? Howard concerned himself with his work. I could put it baldly and say he concerned himself with making money, but Howard wasn't like that. He was a lawyer, and he supported us. He paid for everything we had. He deeply wished things were different in South Africa, and voted for the opposition party in our all-white elections. The opposition had one lone member of parliament, this had gone on for years. A small number of people like Howard and myself voted for them time and time again, and got nowhere. More than that Howard did not feel committed to do, and I agreed. Risking imprisonment or worse was not an option for us. We retained a faint hope that someday, someday, things would change. Howard also considered, over the years, doing the bar exam in New York, and moving us there. He thought — I thought — this was our last option, if no change came.

Why his colleague Jack Benator approached him seeking help with the fugitive lawyer, I cannot say. He probably respected Howard and trusted him; he also knew Howard had the resources and a home where he could help. Jack was not wrong. He, certainly, cannot be blamed.

ONCE, LONG AFTER, Stephen said to Howard, Dad, why, how did you do that, harbour that man, it was such a risky thing to do. Stephen was a lawyer himself then. I didn't hear him ask Howard that, I only know because Howard told me afterwards. I think Stephen knew not to talk about that near me, he just knew. What did you tell him, Howard, I said. I just didn't answer, Howard replied.

EMILY'S HUSBAND, Albert, came and stayed in her room occasionally. He lived in Alexandra township, reached by a long bus ride, where he looked after their three children. I could see the smoke from the coal fires of Alexandra sometimes, on the horizon, I thought I smelled them too. An acrid smell, but a familiar smell. I knew those coal fires, I used to see them along the sides of roads, when we drove to Villiers, my parents' town. Black braziers, red coals glowering through holes, Black men with sticks alongside. Those were on winter days, the sharp, dry winter days when you'd see the yellow-brown veld stretching to the horizon and the sun was pale and distant. So, yes, I knew the smell of coal fires, I knew it.

I don't know where Albert worked, or even if he had a job. Do I feel ashamed that I never knew such things, important things like this? I do feel ashamed. I feel shame, shame over it all. Why did I never ask Emily about her husband's job, Emily who shared so many things with me? I have no answer. It is a failing, a failure, I have to see it now. Not as great a failure as what came after, but a failure nonetheless.

Once there was a loud, unusually loud and continuous barking of the dogs, car doors slamming, men shouting, it must have been three o'clock in the morning. I woke with a start, even Howard woke up, and he slept well. (Dreamless, he claimed, we argued about that once. No one's sleep is dreamless, I said.)

But the shouting early that morning: we knew what it must be. Police, raiding backyards, with their own dogs, in search of people without passes, in the rooms. This happened all the time, we knew it. The sound of it was savage. Dogs, dogs snarling. We'd hear a woman shrieking. They were sounds we knew, in a distant way: the sound of our nights, as we slept in our own bedrooms, in peace. We knew no one would look for us — no police, no dogs, would come for us.

On that morning, in the small hours, we went back to sleep. Perhaps I, myself, did not go straight back to sleep. Perhaps, that is true, I did not.

But first thing, a few short hours later, at eight o'clock, Emily came to my bedroom, my bedroom door. I was still dressing. Ma'am, they took Albert, they took Albert last night. She'd already told Howard, when she served him breakfast at seven, before he left for work.

Albert had no pass to be spending a night in Johannesburg, in the suburbs where we were. Albert, Emily's husband, father of her children. Albert, a tall, gentle man who spoke softly and wore an old-fashioned man's hat with a brim, like my father did.

And that evening, when Howard was home from work, he took Emily in his car and drove to the police station, to bail Albert out of jail. How much did it cost Howard? I have no idea, perhaps very little, perhaps thirty rand — where do I get a number like that? It's lodged in my mind as a memory, a memory of what the bail was. I don't know. Albert was released. He took the bus back to Alexandra township, Howard told me how he dropped him at the stop on Corlett Drive, Albert carrying a small package of his things, his belongings. He wore his hat, as always. Perhaps in his package was some food from Emily, that Emily had taken from our kitchen. I don't know. I remember Howard's face, as he told me.

But this — this was a common occurrence, as I say. It happened all the time. The violence and savagery happened daily, but on our periphery. I mean we, white people: on our periphery.

Emily and Howard drove home from the police station, from the bus stop, Emily sitting in the front — as though they were friends, ordinary friends. Oh, if only to be friends. How do I know Emily sat in the front? I know because that's how it was, how it was with Howard. That, also, is how it was.

AND THERE WAS TINY. Tiny was younger than Emily. She didn't talk much, but she told me that she had two children, they lived in Alexandra too. I think she and Emily helped each other with their families in Alexandra. Taking things for each other, delivering things, passing messages along, on their days off. Now, or here, you would call that a sisterhood, a community, a support system, something like that. I was only vaguely aware of it, I'd hear something between them said in English, or they would tell me.

Emily took the clothes to my children on her day off, ma'am, Tiny would say. Something like that.

ONE AFTERNOON I needed help hanging a small painting. Not one of mine, it was an oil of a Karoo landscape, rocky outcrops, I don't even remember the artist. I was moving it from one small alcove to another in the living room, and needed someone to hold it up for me. Later that evening I would ask Josias to bring his toolbox with hammer and nails, but right then I felt compelled to see it, to see how it would be. At which exact spot it should hang, two inches this way, or two inches that. I went out into the yard to call Tiny. I called and called. The washing line was laden with white sheets, towels, our linens, they moved so slightly in the breeze. The dogs were sleeping, they stirred only briefly at my calling. I could hear the radio from Josias's room. Music, his music, of course.

Tiny emerged at last from her room, from her low door, she was straightening her *doek,* her head scarf. Yes ma'am? she said. I think, or I felt, then, that there was a man, a friend, in her room. A lover. I don't know. I felt it. I felt stupid and cruel for bothering her on her afternoon rest. I said, never mind, never mind Tiny, just a small thing, a small thing it is, we can do it later. And we did, we hung the picture later. I return to that memory so often. Perhaps for the first time I thought, or felt, Tiny had her own, intimate, life. She was a young woman after all. How had that not occurred to me before?

JOSEPH HAD BEEN in the garden room for a few weeks. I never saw him, or heard him. Some days I thought we'd imagined him, perhaps he wasn't really there. I think for the children it was like that: a suggestion of a person, but not a real person. I don't think they thought of him, at all. Now that strikes me as strange, but I think it's true.

I had an idea Joseph emerged at night, when we were all asleep, perhaps he walked around the garden. He'd need exercise, he'd need to stretch his legs. I thought how quiet it must be down there under the trees at night; only Joseph. There was an old white bench set back under a willow tree, I imagined it glimmering in the soft dark, and perhaps Joseph had found it and would sit there, listening to the silence, breathing the night air.

I thought about this, worried about it, as I walked, myself, through my day. Up and down the garden; to the pool; to my car. I didn't walk much.

But Joseph. He was like a prisoner. He *was* a prisoner.

I had no idea about his wife and children, but he'd mentioned them. He'd told Howard and me, that first evening, that his mother-in-law had moved into his house, she would help. I tried to imagine them: people like us, but alone now at home, without him. How they managed for money, I don't know. Perhaps the resistance, the organization, paid for his family, that might be so. Perhaps his family was living on saved money, he'd been a lawyer, after all. Again, I don't know.

I did know that his colleagues, his comrades, visited him late at night. He had told us this would happen, and soon enough Emily had told me about it. She said men, two or three men, came every night, around midnight, they let themselves in the back gate, walked through the servants' yard, into the garden, and down, down, to the end of the garden, to his room. She told me the dogs' barking woke her, every time, they woke Josias and Tiny too, but they all knew what it was, so they simply went back to sleep. Two or so hours later the men would leave, the same way, dogs barking again, and they'd all be woken, once more.

I imagined it: the blackness of night, and a car pulling up, its engine turned off, its pooling lights. Perhaps the car pulled up two or three doors away, and parked in a different place each night. They wouldn't do things exactly the same each time, and take the risk of being noticed.

The three men, or two men, shadows, would make their way along the pavement, against our white walls, one of them carrying dinner, food, for Joseph in our garden. As I imagined it. What would the dinner be? I did worry about what he ate, I worried about that from the beginning. Perhaps they picked up something from the Indian take-away at the other end of Corlett Drive, I think they did that. A curry and rice. Coca-Cola to drink, paper cups. Paper and plastic utensils. And they'd crowd into his low room, only one chair to sit on — standing, then, or sitting on the bed, or the floor.

And then, to work: plans rolled out. A white map. Discussions, arguments, late into the night, under the dim light bulb. It was summer then, the months of summer, there would be moths against his light, moths batting their frail wings against his light.

Sometimes I wished I could be there, to hear what they were saying. I imagined Joseph's silver-rimmed glasses, his dark hair. I felt deep respect. And then I felt moved. These feelings accompanied my days, then. They were new, there was a new space now, in my mind. A space for the work they were doing, for the respect I felt.

I think Howard felt the same, although he never said much. Just: everything okay with the garden room? Yes, yes, all fine, I'd say.

And the servants. How could they believe he was a 'friend come to stay'? They spoke, I saw now, more quietly among themselves, in their own language. I wonder what they said. Perhaps they understood. They knew there was a resistance, of course they knew. Now they understood the resistance had come here, right here, behind our whitewashed walls, beside our glittering swimming pool, under the trees, to the end of our garden. They understood.

And this was why I now told Emily not to tell anyone, anyone she knew. It was a secret, that's all I said. And tell Josias and Tiny, I said. She looked at me. Alright ma'am, she said. It's alright. Perhaps I was trembling a little, when I told her that, I felt myself to be quite pale. I went to my room to lie down. This had become more than we'd thought. I remember that afternoon. It took me a while to calm down before I lay on my bed, I remember my face in my mirror, my dressing table mirror. It was pale, against my smooth dark hair.

Once, in New York, Helena, eleven years old, had a friend to play, they spent the afternoon whispering in her room, I remember it. I was busy with my things — in the living room, perhaps I was reading — but I kept thinking, what are they whispering about. Ordinary things, of course ordinary things, little girls' things. There'd be giggling, then gales of laughter, then silence again and the sound of things being moved in the room. And when they came out I said, girls, what are you whispering about, I said it good-humouredly of course, and Helena said, it's a secret, a secret. And her friend said, we have a secret, shhhhhhhh . . . and they laughed together, again.

There are small, harmless secrets, innocent secrets, and then there are large, important secrets. I remember thinking that, then. And I remember feeling guilty about the large, important secret we'd had in our house in Johannesburg: the large, important secret that begat other secrets. *Don't tell anyone, remember,* I had said to Emily. *Don't tell anyone.*

MY PARENTS CAME for a short visit from Villiers, it was a long weekend. Klaas, who worked for my father, drove them. They came in their blue Peugeot, I remember Josias calling, calling through the house when they arrived. The dogs barked, the children were so excited, there was Emily laughing with Klaas as she greeted him, and the cling peaches in their cardboard box — pale orange — like a blessing.

My parents brought other things too, they always did. My mother had a new, smaller throw she'd made, to put over a chair, and she'd brought her bag with the tortoiseshell handle, filled with a new knitting project, a sweater this time, for Stephen. She worked on it on the patio through the days she was visiting. I picture her now there, alone under the white trellis. She avoided the sun.

My father smoked a pipe, he left trails of ash wherever he went, and kept bags of tobacco in his pockets. He and Howard shared interests in business, my father had a shop, a wholesale business, in his town. He was a man of great energy then, with a booming voice. He and Howard talked about the stock market, about the price of gold. Anglo American, De Beers. The price of shares. I didn't understand any of that, or care.

But I felt, as always, the weight that an only child carries. The weight of my parents' lives. I still feel it now sometimes, and they are long gone.

My parents slept in our spare room, it had two single beds, narrow, how I remember the room, filled then with their suitcases, they seemed to bring so much.

The problem was, that visit, we had the man — Joseph — in the garden. This was a large, an unprecedented, problem.

I HAD TRIED to dissuade my mother from coming. I told her Howard was very busy at work and tired, that I had been under the weather. This was a mistake, to say that, because my mother was, at once, alarmed. Then I must come, she said. I can help you. Oh, no, no, I said. Mom, I have Emily. But she wouldn't be dissuaded. I tried again, with a different excuse. We've been painting the spare room, I said, it's a mess. Why are you doing that, my mother said, the room's lovely as it is. She really wanted to come. She had peaches to deliver, the new sweater for Stephen was almost finished. They came.

They stayed for three days and two nights. I had to lie, and say we'd postponed the room painting. My mother was unconcerned. She said, again, it's a lovely room, leave it as it is.

I remember every minute of those three days and two nights, because we were keeping a secret. I thought, with renewed clarity, of the absurdity of it: a man in our garden.

But my mother never strayed far from the house, or from the patio, where she'd sit under the shading trellis with her handwork, her knitting. From there she could watch the children swimming. They liked it, and showed off especially then: their swim strokes, their skills. There was Helena in a new green swimsuit, my mother admiring it. The children would dash up to the patio, wet and shaking water off themselves, like dogs, and they'd eat something, Emily would have made tea and a cake, a poppy seed cake, or a lemon loaf. My mother enjoyed all this, that's why she had come, after all. I had a sense of her loneliness at home in her town, on her red-floored porch with her cacti. Maggie, her maid, in the yard.

Maggie had worked for my mother for a long time, but

Maggie had a problem with drink. Perhaps having Maggie gave my mother something to do, someone to mother, I see it now, these years later. I didn't see it then, because I remember people — my mother's neighbour — urging my mother to get rid of Maggie, she's lazy, why keep her on, they'd say. But my mother kept Maggie.

She drove her to the doctor once a month, where Maggie was prescribed medication, I think the medication helped the drinking, what medication exactly it was I don't know. But it helped. Maggie would be fine for a while: she, my mother's companion, pottering in the kitchen over the sink, the dishes, sweeping and tidying.

Then she'd start drinking again. My mother would notice small changes: a new, vague, look in Maggie's eyes, a vase misplaced, even broken, something like that. Soon enough, Maggie would come into the kitchen an hour late, the smell of meths from her, unmistakable.

MY MOTHER had never been down to the end of the garden at our house, or seen my studio. No one had. That's how I wanted it. It was my room, my studio: my own, sacred, space. Anyone who came to our house knew that.

My father, too, never went farther than the edge of the swimming pool, never walked down the hill to the end of the garden. It's only once that I remember him at the pool, when Howard had showed him something with the filter, with the chlorine. My father knew nothing about that, but Howard was being a host, showing a guest his home and preoccupations, I suppose.

During my parents' visit I myself never went into my studio, I never worked on my painting. How could I? I was busy too, being a host. Mostly I was in the kitchen, unusual for me, talking with Emily about the next meal, what should be served, checking that Emily had everything, did I need to phone an order in to the grocer for this or that? That's how I did our food shopping, then. I'd phone our corner grocer, I'd say, it's Mrs. Kline here. Yes ma'am, hello ma'am, she'd say. And I'd give my order: a dozen eggs, please, two loaves of bread, a pound of butter, a bag of sugar, my usual, and the other usual things, please. Then I'd do the same with the butcher. And they'd deliver it, Josias carrying in the bags, large, heavy bags, through the back gate, into the kitchen. I've said before: food didn't interest me much.

My mother wouldn't have seen Emily go down with a food tray to the garden room in the mornings, because Emily went down early, before eight, earlier than my parents got up. I imagine Emily took care at the end of the day not to go down again, to pick up his dishes, until my mother was no longer on the patio.

I don't really know how everyone else felt that weekend. The children had a secret which they never told, for them it was a habit, an old habit, from early days, of not talking to their grandparents about politics. A habit they had picked up, as if by osmosis, from me and Howard.

Howard was his usual relaxed and preoccupied self, and he liked my parents. He enjoyed my father's company, it was a pleasant weekend for him. Years later, here, he said once, out of the blue: the weekend your parents came? I knew, right away, which weekend he meant, how was it we never talked about it, yet it was so close to my thoughts, even then? My God, he said. We never talked of it again.

So I have an idea it was I, alone, who suffered that weekend. I don't think I slept. I, who've often had trouble sleeping. I remember getting up and dressing, looking in my mirror, in the morning light. A pallor, again. I smoothed and brushed my hair. My mother commented, several times, on my pallor. I told you I've been under the weather, I said, fighting a cold. I drank a glass of orange juice that I had Emily squeeze, I never drank orange juice. Vitamin C, my mother said. But I don't think she was convinced, or reassured.

I WONDERED HOW my parents' visit disturbed Joseph. If it disturbed him. I imagined his days: still and quiet in his room, shadows from the trees and leaves falling on the stone floor, through the two small windows. His light on, he reading at his table. Reading, reading. Of course, he must be reading. Like a monk. I wondered what he'd be wearing, it was still summer. I knew his friends, his comrades, were taking and washing his clothes, and returning them. I had told Emily, one day, to ask if he had laundry. No, no, he said. My friends will do it. Emily told me this after. Perhaps Emily found it all as unsettling — as strange — as I did, but she didn't say. Not then, she didn't say then. In any case, I doubt Joseph had or wore many clothes, I mean, beyond a shirt, pants, his shoes and socks. I didn't think further. He told Emily his friends would take care of his bedsheets and towels too.

Again, I pictured him. His reading. I felt kindred to him, perhaps he was like me. A solitary person, living in his own mind. I assumed his comrades brought him books and things he had to read, I knew, by instinct, that these were as important to him as the food Emily brought, every day. He was, indeed, like me.

THE VISIT FROM MY PARENTS ended. Nothing I feared about Joseph being discovered happened. I remember the goodbyes, the children jumping up and down as Klaas loaded the car, how many suitcases for such a short visit! The dogs jumping and wagging their tails, they knew my parents too. Klaas joking and talking in Xhosa with Josias, Josias even smiling, almost laughing, for once. Klaas had slept in Josias's room, they made their own arrangements about that. Of course, now, only now, it occurs to me: what bedding did they use? Perhaps Klaas brought a blanket with him, all the way from Villiers in the car, and slept on the stone floor, under it. I think that might be what they did. I remember hearing Klaas talking in the back room of the kitchen, late, when the servants were eating their dinner, their stew and *mieliepap*, their radio with music on. It was an enjoyable visit for them too. We — they — had all known Klaas for a while.

I DID COME DOWN with a cold. On the Tuesday after my parents' visit. I think I was . . . shattered . . . by the collision of the two worlds, the world of my parents, and Joseph in our garden room. And in our own home. It didn't feel like my home any more. I felt so ill, I became fevered. I retired, I retired to my room, to my bed.

For one week I lay in my room, curtains drawn. I'd never drawn my curtains during the day. The room, now, was dim. I lay under my covers, how I remember it. Emily brought me thin gruels she had made, on her tray, I barely touched them. In the afternoons she'd bring me tea, with lemon. I hardly drank that. She brought plates of dry toast, she tried that, but I didn't eat.

Helena was taken to ballet classes that week by her friend's mother, and she and Stephen walked to school, down the street, they had never needed me to drive them. What else went on in the house while I was sick, I don't know. Emily did everything as usual, and directed Tiny. Josias did his work, as usual, I am sure. Howard came home every evening and came straight to my room, he'd bend down over the bed to kiss me on my forehead, and ask worriedly, are you feeling better, are you feeling better yet?

Every evening, my mother would call. I didn't want to speak to her but Howard said I must, I must speak to her, she'd think there was something really wrong otherwise. I'd finally pick up the black phone receiver next to my bed, Howard would have been talking to her, in hushed tones, on the receiver in his study. I'd hear her thin voice over the wire, perhaps plaintive now. I'll be fine, Mom, I said, just a cold, just a bad cold, that's all. I could hear my voice, as I said it. A soft voice I have, I think, but it had a note of uncertainty in it now, I could hear it.

My painting, its luminousness, retreated, it went away as I lay sick. I thought, briefly, I might lose it and not find it again. This filled me with a sudden, bleak, despair. For an instant I felt bereft, as though something crucial to me, or someone, had died. Perhaps, then, I slept.

I'd wake, and remember again the two rooms, the two garden rooms, because there were two now. His; and mine. I thought of my own, the studio, I thought of it as abandoned, the many canvases stacked and idle, abandoned brushes, the paints in their tubes, unopened ones, and used ones, bent and twisted, some fallen to the stone floor. And his room: he. Was he still reading, and reading, as before? The thought brought me pain. I imagined his bent, dark head. I felt, then, deep compassion for him, for his situation. I tried, I tried again, to forget about it, put it out of mind. And then I'd sleep, again.

Emily and Howard were alarmed, they were alarmed I didn't eat. Howard called the doctor. Sidney was our family doctor, he lived not far away. He came, he listened to my chest, he took my temperature. It's really just a cold, he said. Just a cold. Drink fluids. Take aspirin to bring the fever down, go to sleep. I will, I said. I will. I didn't, I didn't take aspirin. I've mentioned before: I've never taken a drug.

I recovered. I emerged at last from my room. We opened the curtains. Emily made my bed with new linens. I was weak, and thinner, but I was fine. I promised Howard I would eat and gain weight, and Emily now brought me glasses of cold milk on her tray. The milk was full-cream, we had it delivered in bottles every morning, I remember the cream on top, and the silver foil seal that was its lid. I've not seen milk like that since. The milk tasted so pure. Like a time long ago. I drank; I drank milk. In the evenings Emily warmed it, and brought me a cup, the milk warm with tiny bubbles. Perhaps I'd not had milk to drink since my childhood, perhaps that is true.

But I didn't go near my studio, I was almost afraid. I felt that I might not find my painting there, that it might be vanished.

A COUPLE OF WEEKS LATER, Howard and I were invited to a party. We had invitations to parties often, but we didn't often accept them. Should I say, I didn't often accept them. Howard would happily have gone, but I didn't like parties, sometimes they ruffled me terribly, for days afterwards. The noise, and the obligations, the obligations to speak to people and present a good face, I felt it a great strain.

Howard warned me, this time. Jack Benator, Howard's colleague and partner, who had arranged Joseph's stay at our house, would be at the party. I knew Jack, but had not seen him since Joseph had come to stay with us.

The party was on a patio under the stars, and next to a swimming pool, glinting blackly under the lights. There were drinks, and canapés. Music. I remember my shoulders were bare, it was summer still. I would have been drinking a glass of white wine, perhaps a lime and soda, I imagine its coolness, its ice, the glass against my hand.

And then Jack Benator was in front of me. I smiled at him, briefly, hello. He nodded. Then he looked into my face searchingly, and said, how are you? I understood at once this to be a question about Joseph, a veiled question, and I felt a stab — now familiar — of alarm. Oh, fine, thanks, I said. Then I added, as he continued looking at me, everything's just fine. No problem. He nodded. Then he turned away.

We had communicated about our secret. That's how it was.

There were other things that went on at those parties, they interested me not at all. A particular man I remember came over to me, his wife was across the patio. Beautiful dress, dear, he said to me, looking down at my shoulders. I even remember my dress, which was plain white, its straps were green. It was a dress my mother had made, I'd worn it many times. Have I said how my mother made dresses? She would have made many more dresses for me, had I let her. The man said then, in a very low voice, so that only I could hear him, pretty girl, he said, pretty girl. I was filled with revulsion; I turned away. I went to find Howard. Please, please, can we go home, I said. We did, we did go home. I didn't even tell Howard what happened, but Howard understood me, as I've said many times.

WE WENT, OCCASIONALLY, to spend a weekend with my parents in Villiers. We'd leave Josias at the white garage door, hauling it shut as he waved goodbye, then Howard would drive — out of the city, to the highway. We'd reach the yellow mine dumps then, that circled the city, perhaps that was the rare time I had a sense of our city, of what it was, what it actually was. A city born on a seam of gold, deep in the earth: a seam of gold. The mines would be there, I couldn't see them from the car, but I imagined them: black and blacked with coal, with coal fires; iron and massive, and the men, the men, of course, the lines of Black men, many of them, who went down, in black elevators, into the earth. Without those men, the gold would never be mined. Anglo American and the gold shares; the Johannesburg stock exchange; none of them would exist without that manpower, those men.

We'd hear of mine accidents, sometimes they were reported in the papers. Mostly, they were not. I would notice, right away, if there was a small report, a small column in the bottom corner of the third page: Mine explosion on West Rand, Randfontein mine. Eighty-seven dead. Like that. I know, now, that there were many such accidents, many such deaths. The death of a young Black man, newly arrived in Johannesburg to work on the gold mine, one young Black man. I'd put it out of mind. I think about that often now. One young Black man. Dead. Another one. Of course you — you, an American — will know I am reminded of it every day, over here: dead Black men, every day, here. Not in gold mines, not in gold mines. But it comes to the same thing. It's the same thing.

Helena has asked me about that. How many Black men died in mine accidents over the years, do you know, Mom? I don't know, Helena, I said, but many. And not only in mine accidents, I said. You can find it in books, history books, I told her. She knows that; perhaps she's spent many hours poring over such books, in that library near Waterbury, where she lives. I think she has.

DRIVING TO VILLIERS, we'd pass Vereeniging, Vanderbijlpark, then we'd see signs for other towns: Sasolburg, Viljoenskroon... and then we'd be on the veld.

It stretched, a dun colour, to the sky. We'd pass some signs, now and then, again: Vredefort, Steynsrus, Ventersburg. Some black electricity pylons. Nothing, nothing else, just flatness, as far as you could see.

The names of other towns: Abrahamsrust, Tweeling. I didn't think the veld beautiful then, but it is beautiful as I think of it now. I thought it was brown and featureless, that's what I thought.

I never painted the veld. I never painted landscapes much. But you know that.

We'd come upon the river then, the Vaal River. It was a brown river, and very wide, wider than anything I knew. There were pale trees that grew alongside, for many miles, but more often no trees — no green — at all. The highway followed the river, the river's slow route. Once we drove to Villiers after the river had flooded, it flooded sometimes, when the great rains came. A brown stream, overflowing its banks, breaking its banks, we knew, then, its power.

SUMMER HAD ADVANCED, Joseph in the room for several more weeks, now. I'd still not seen him since the first evening, the first morning.

But my painting had receded further from me, I'd not worked on it.

Eric at the art shop didn't see me for a while. Or, I didn't see him. I'd think about him from time to time. Perhaps he was worried about me. Perhaps I'd go in again one day, I thought. But what would I say to him? He genuinely cared about my painting, it would hurt him, too, to hear what had happened, what had happened between me and my painting.

One day on the patio, as I was having lunch and looking down into the trees, thinking of Joseph and his room, invisible there, I thought perhaps I'd go and knock on his door. Perhaps that might make me feel better about everything. Perhaps, after that, I could go into my studio and see my painting again. Start work on it again.

Perhaps Joseph would welcome a visitor.

What possessed me? I don't know.

I stood up. I started walking down the grass. It was a beautiful day, the trees hung, hung, as they always did, and rustled, just a little, as I walked. I walked down the small hill, I walked in my sandals, I remember the sandals. And then I was there, his room in front of me. I thought then it was a beautiful structure, so plain, its stone grey, a small symmetrical cottage, with two windows that weren't large, surrounded by deep trees. That's all.

Nothing stirred, I could have been a small animal. There was the worn stone step. The door was a low one, old wood, whitewashed. It had a round knob, also worn, the kind that turned. I imagined it would make a sound, a sound of the metal against metal, inside its mechanism, a small, small, sound.

But then, I stopped. I'd heard the dogs barking up in the yard, they had broken the silence, the spell. Because a spell it was. I stood for one more moment, perhaps Joseph would come out? But no. I turned around quickly and walked, very fast, up the hill. I hastened, under the trees, past the patio, my abandoned lunch on its white plate, into the house, into the dark passage, and walked quickly, quickly, to my room. And then I was there.

I shut the door behind me, and stood with my back against it, breathing, I remember my breathing. And then I went to my dressing table. I saw my face in the mirror. It was flushed, I never had a flushed face. I remember my eyes.

It took me a while to calm myself, I paced back and forth, back and forth, in front of the dressing table, the mirror, and in front of the window, where I looked, again, into the garden, so green.

And then, finally, I lay down, for my afternoon rest. But those afternoons no longer had my painting in them, in my mind. My mind, now, was blank.

L ATER THAT DAY I asked Emily, in the kitchen, how Joseph was doing. Was everything alright with him, I said. Ja, is fine, Emily said. He eats all the food, that's how I know he's fine. He eats the scrambled eggs, the toast, in the morning, and I leave him bread and cheese and butter, for lunch. Everything gone when I come again at night, she said. That's good, that's good. Thank you, Emily, I said. Thank you.

But ma'am, she said. She looked up then from her wooden board, she was chopping things, vegetables, for dinner. I could see she didn't know how to carry on. She put her knife down. Ma'am. I stand on the step when he opens the door, she said, and I see, behind him I see, is his table, his small table you put there. There's papers, pages on the table, many pages. There's also books, books piled next to the table, on the floor. He has a pen always in his hand, even when he's opening the door for me. His light is on, even though it's daytime. I see this is because he's reading. And writing. And he's wearing his glasses, you know his glasses, ma'am. Yes, Emily, I said, I know. And he's wearing, you know, the same clothes, the same shirt, every day, she went on. Once I see he changed his shirt, only one time. But he's a very clean man, you saw that also, ma'am, you saw that. Yes, Emily, yes, I saw that. Ah, Emily said, and she shook her head. Is not good situation, she said. Yes, Emily, that is true, I said. We stood, the two of us, at her board, the kitchen counter: Emily's place; her domain. Thank you, Emily, I said, and I went to my room. But my room was no longer a refuge, it no longer felt calm.

And sometime after that Emily reported to me Joseph's light bulb had gone out, he needed another. I had Josias fetch one from the garage and give it to Emily, to take down, next time. I worried about the light for his eyes, I knew it wasn't really an adequate light, at all.

And another day I said to Emily, because it was bothering me: you know what work he's doing there, don't you, Emily? She looked at me, then looked away. Yes ma'am, I know, I know what it is. He's a good man, ma'am. A good man. Yes, he is, I said. I felt close to tears.

I WENT TO VISIT ERIC at his store. He was happy to see me; I was happy to see him too. But then he said: you look very thin, have you been alright? Where've you been? Oh, Eric, I was a bit sick, yes. But I'm fine. Not painting though. Eric knew this was not a good thing, not good at all. He looked concerned. Look, will you have some tea, he said, I'm boiling water now. I had tea with Eric.

We sat up on high stools near his cash register at the front of the store. He brought me tea in a mug. Black please, I said. His was milky. We shared a plate of biscuits, perhaps I had one biscuit. Eric was still working on his own portfolio, he showed me some new things. Every week he'd bring out a work-in-progress, and prop it up against one of the easels, and we'd both stand back then, and study it, and I'd comment. His work was becoming more refined over time, I could see that. Just keep going, I'd say, this is the right direction you're moving in. It's good, it's good.

AND SO tea with Eric, in 1972, became a highlight of my week. His store was dusty, and full of stacks and stacks of stretched canvases, against the walls. Then there were the stacks of wooden frames, and stretcher bars. There were his shelves of paints, tubes and tubes of them; then brushes; palette knives.

We talked and talked.

Eric had said he'd teach me to stretch my own canvases, then I could do it myself at home. I used to watch him doing it, a long procedure with many careful steps. Most artists do it themselves, he said. You have more flexibility that way, make different sizes whenever you want, that kind of thing.

No, no, I said, I don't want to, I'll just buy them stretched here. I didn't trust myself and perhaps I was even a bit lazy that way: a whole extra set of steps to follow, pieces of wood, the measuring. I wouldn't do that. Eric primed my canvases for me too, although he'd suggested I could do that myself also. (In later years I always primed my own canvases, and stretched them too.)

We talked about artists we admired, South African artists. We spoke of David Goldblatt, the photographer just making a name for himself, then. If the subject of politics came up — and how could it not — Eric would swear, terrible expletives, he'd just swear. He was speechless with fury. As I was, but in a more measured and quiet way. So we steered away from that subject, and it never occurred to me, in a million years, to mention the man in our garden room.

And I encouraged Eric with his work, I felt protective of him. I was just a bit older than him. He talked about his struggles, how art school had been an inspiration for him. I'd not gone to art school, I'd studied history of art at university, I think you know that.

At university I spent hours in the library looking at images of paintings — pale imitations — in books. Hours and hours poring over those images, and later I bought my own books with colour plates. I kept them in my studio, piled haphazardly on a small table near the window. *Velázquez: Las Meninas. The self-portraits of Rembrandt. Manet's Black.*

It seemed to me that *Las Meninas* contained all the light, but especially, the darkness — that darkness he achieved with black, shades of black. The layers and depth on the canvas, in the canvas. The room portrayed in that painting; its mirror. There was the girl in a white dress. Perhaps I was the girl in a white dress.

Velázquez knew everything.

AFTER UNIVERSITY I found Jocelyn. Jocelyn Turner, the art teacher who became my mentor. Without her — without Jocelyn — I would be nothing. I think so. She guided me, as I worked towards my own . . . language, my own painting language. I'd sit in her workroom, it was a room flooded with white light, its high windows, we could see the tall trees of her garden, moving, leaves touched by the slight breeze. Long afternoons spent at the wooden table, that long worktable. And Jocelyn's voice, she had a soft voice.

At Jocelyn's worktable I learned the feel of paper, different kinds of paper. Rougher paper, or finer, or heavier and thicker paper. More textured.

I learned the exactness of a pigment: cadmium yellow. Ivory black, and carbon black. The whites: titanium, zinc, and the best one, lead. Lead white, or flake white. The colour most often on my palette, later.

In my memories Jocelyn's room is a soundscape, the sound, that rustling sound of paper, or of graphite — pencil — moving on paper. The small sound of a jar of turpentine set down on the wooden table, a faint setting down. And the brushstrokes on canvas, such a soft sound, if you used a large, flat brush. Or perhaps I just imagine I heard that, because mostly you don't hear brushstrokes.

You don't hear paint. Or perhaps you do.

I learned the techniques of oil, the layering. I learned about underpainting, that first, original layer. The one on which the whole work, all the next layers, are built.

I learned how long it takes for oil paint to dry, for the layers, for each layer, to dry. It takes a long time.

WITH JOCELYN, under Jocelyn's guidance, I moved from figurative work towards abstraction. Over time, it no longer interested me to represent things. I became more interested in textures, in pure colours, in the rhythm underlying the canvas, or the rhythm and tone underlying things, something like that.

Abstraction was dominant in South African art during the 1960s and '70s, you probably know this. Jocelyn had paintings by George Boys, Lionel Abrams, other abstract artists. Howard and I once bought a Lionel Abrams from her because I admired it so much. It was ochre-coloured, and large, it was in our dining room, it was made of planes of pure colour, planes and planes: sienna, burnt umber, across the canvas.

I thought that abstraction was . . . a path I could follow. I would never have made protest art — what is called protest art. Protest art was too direct for me, I think you understand that.

ONCE OR TWICE Eric invited me to the opening of an art show, he followed things like that, although I didn't. I went with Howard, and I remember the first time they met, a winter's night when we arrived, in jackets, at a small gallery, and I saw Eric at the end of the room, with a drink.

My husband, Howard, I said, as I introduced them. And this is Eric, I said, my champion! The man in my art shop. Ah, said Howard, gracious Howard. I know how important you are then, he said. Eric bowed in a mock-formal way. We all laughed. We looked at the work, they were charcoals, all black-and-white, a young Black artist, a man from Soweto. It was a joy to be there. I remember Eric and Howard's faces, as they spoke about this work, this figure, this particular line, or that one. At moments like that, I felt myself blessed.

PERHAPS ERIC was the only one who knew I was struggling with my painting those early months of 1972. Jocelyn was old and became ill, I no longer had lessons with her. And I never told Howard about the struggle, I simply couldn't. It was too close, too intimate, to talk about my painting — with him. So I didn't.

Perhaps Howard thought I was going into my studio every day, as before. I don't know. Probably Emily and Josias noticed I wasn't in my studio any more, but what did this mean to them? Emily knew I painted pictures, but she'd never asked me anything about it, never even asked to see what I did. Which is strange, as I think about it now.

I didn't tell Eric the whole of it, how could I? That would have meant telling him about Joseph in the garden room, and I wasn't going to do that. I said I had a block, sometimes we laughed about it. You're not a writer, you know, he'd say. Writers have blocks. I laughed. Well, it's a block, I said, and that's that. Every block becomes unblocked at some point, he said. I'd carry his words with me as I drove, wound my way through the quiet streets, home.

AND TINY. Tiny had been learning, following Emily around and doing her work. But one morning Emily came in, she came right to my bedroom again, as she did when something was wrong. Ma'am, she said. Ma'am. Tiny is sick. Tiny must go to the hospital. Please come, ma'am. I followed her out right away, I was still in my dressing gown. Tiny was sitting in a chair at the back of the kitchen, where the three of them ate. There were their plates of food, breakfast, large slabs of bread, tea steaming in mugs. Tiny's face was swollen, her one eye was swollen. I could see a bruise starting on her neck. She was crying quietly. What happened, what happened, I said. Josias, standing nearby, clicked his tongue, and shook his head. Emily looked embarrassed. Tiny cried into her sleeve, then she covered her face with both hands, as if in shame. It took a few minutes to get it out of them, but Tiny had a boyfriend, and it was he who was responsible. I remembered, then, the afternoon when I had disturbed Tiny in her room, on her break. I felt furious. But furious with whom?

I called Sidney, our doctor, and he came to see her. He examined her carefully in the kitchen, gave her cold compresses and aspirin, and said nothing, although to me he said, Jacqueline, this is really not in order, you know. There's a limit to what you can do for these people, there's a limit. Yes, Sidney, I said, thank you for seeing her. I know. I know how it is. Goodbye.

IT HAPPENED AGAIN, a couple of weeks later. Sidney was called once more.

We all spoke to Tiny: I, Emily, even Josias. I heard Josias talking in a low voice to her, in their language. He's not a good boyfriend, I said. Please get rid of him, I said. I'm sure Emily said the same.

Emily was worried about Tiny's children in Alexandra, what would happen to them if the boyfriend killed her one day, she said. Don't exaggerate, Emily, I said.

But Tiny carried on with her boyfriend. Once, only once, I saw him. He was a tall, thin man, and young. He walked casually through the back gate and into their yard, I was in the yard that day, that's why I saw him. He walked past me, insolently, he looked at me as he walked, and then he walked straight to Tiny's room, bending his head as he went through the low doorway.

I ASKED HOWARD that night if he thought we should let Tiny go, perhaps it wasn't safe for us to have this man in our backyard, visiting regularly. What did Howard think? Should we call the police next time he assaults her, I said.

But we were all afraid of the police, you see that now. I was afraid of the police for our own reason, Joseph in the garden, and Tiny was afraid of the police because her boyfriend didn't have a pass, and now, Tiny told us tearfully, she didn't have a pass either. When I hired her, I hadn't bothered to check, sometimes I was careless that way. How could I have made that mistake? But it was my kind of rebellion, to make that mistake. I hated those passes, I hated that system,

I just hated it. When Tiny came to my door looking for a job, she caught me at a moment when I needed someone, and I was preoccupied I suppose in my way, and rebellious, that too, and I thought Tiny looked suitable. She was young and soft-spoken. I hired her.

She didn't have a pass. We couldn't call the police.

This was a rare time Howard was angry with me. What the hell, he said. Now look what's happened. But then he said, almost immediately: look, we'll keep her on, it's her job. Maybe I'll talk to the boyfriend.

I didn't think this was a good idea, not at all. Emily and Josias shook their heads when I told them, they surely didn't think it was a good idea, either.

HOWARD LATER CAME into the kitchen. Tiny, he said, next time your boyfriend comes please call me, tell him I want to talk to him. Tiny looked frightened, then she smiled uncertainly. Okay master, thank you master, she said, and she went out the back, to her room.

Nothing happened for several days. And then, one morning, Emily knocked on my door, and I tied my dressing gown belt and hurried after her to the kitchen, to find Tiny, bruised and crying, again. Why didn't you call Howard, I said, why? She cried, she covered her face with her hands.

Sidney came. He left the compresses and aspirin, he made a cold comment again, to me. He left. I watched him walk away from the front door, carrying his black doctor's bag, on his way to his car, to another patient. A more legitimate patient, he no doubt thought. I knew Sidney's way of thinking. A white child with a sore throat, tonsilitis, nothing more, something like that. That's how it was.

Howard, I think, washed his hands of it, he said no more about it. He left it, I suppose, to me. To manage the backyard and the servants, and Tiny, whom I, after all, had carelessly hired. Perhaps it wouldn't happen again.

Except one day Tiny disappeared. I mean, she was no longer in her room at the back, she had taken her things with her too. Emily was as shocked as we were. She was upset for days. Emily sent word to Alexandra, to the house where Tiny's children lived. But they had not seen Tiny, either.

I went to see Tiny's room. The iron bed, elevated on bricks, two under each of the four legs. The thin mattress, its bedding gone too. The upside-down milkcrates that served as her table. The concrete floor. That's all.

Howard went to the local police station this time. He gave them her name; he said she was a friend of his maid. He didn't — couldn't — say she worked for us. I followed up with calls to the police station, every day. I spoke, each time, to a desultory young man, who sounded bored. No ma'am, he said. No ma'am, no information.

Tiny had only been with us a short while.

But a disappeared woman, what does that mean?

O THERWISE our domestic routine, and the children's routines, carried on as before.

Emily told me that she talked to Joseph in the garden room from time to time, now. I feel for him, ma'am, she said. I was surprised.

What does he tell you, Emily, I said. She was stirring in a mixing bowl, I remember, because Helena was there, agitating, asking about a cake, what kind of cake would Emily make, today. Wait, wait, patience! Emily said. Helena ran off. What does he say, Emily? I said. He said he is so grateful for all this, for this room, ma'am. He told me he goes with the comrades in the car at night, they go to Soweto, his other friends, his comrades are there. We are working, working, you know that? That's what he told me, ma'am.

Emily was pleased, I was pleased, to hear he left the room at night. He was less imprisoned, then. I suddenly felt less imprisoned, myself.

And now, at night, as I lay and heard the faint barking of the dogs, I'd picture them, three, or two shadows, he and his comrades walking through the garden, up the hill, past the pool, through the yard, out the back gate, creaking on its hinge, they even laughing quietly. Perhaps.

Free. For the moment, free.

Then to the car, into the car, the engine purring into life, the lights pooling, and pulling away. Away, down Corlett Drive, through the city, deserted now, just street lights, and the long drive to Soweto, on the distant side of the city. Another car's red tail-lights blinking ahead.

And then: rutted roads, no street lights. A different place.

Soweto. And there, walking along a warren of laneways, rutted all, behind and between, and ducking into a small, small house, filled with men, only men. Then: embraced, Joseph embraced by his comrades, his colleagues. Handshakes, and laughing. Reassurances of safety. And beer, beers opened. Smoking, a haze of smoke in the room. And finally: the charts, the papers, the maps. Down to work.

Plotting the overthrow of our country's government. Plotting and planning the overthrow of our lives.

I pictured him, then: his glasses, his bearded face, his smile. Alive, and free. I almost wept with the relief of it.

And then in the early hours of the morning, perhaps four o'clock, the car driving back, out of Soweto and its acrid coal fire-smell, the morning coal fires, the commuters, lines of Black people already at the buses, and towards us, to the dark and distant suburbs, where we were. And dropping Joseph off, down the street, as he'd walk, quickly, to our gate. He'd let himself in by that old latch, walk quickly, quickly, down the grass, to his room, that small stone room. And he'd reach, at last, his bed. His narrow bed with its old springs, that I could see, could hear, so clearly in my mind.

I thought they must be white people who came in the car, it would have been too risky for Black people to be seen by the police coming into our neighbourhood, driving to Soweto and back, and at night. They must have had it all so carefully planned. I was amazed, as I thought about it. Thanks for telling me, Emily, I said, I am glad to hear it, glad he goes out. Don't tell anyone, remember. Yes ma'am, I know that, ma'am, she'd say.

I DIDN'T KNOW IF Joseph saw his wife or children. I thought perhaps he did not. I knew it wasn't safe for him to be taken to his house, where they were.

Stories have been told, books written, about those families, the families of activists, who were left behind. I've read some of them. You, you can read them too. They are hard to read.

Perhaps I felt calmer for a few weeks. There was a space where Tiny had been, we struggled with that.

Howard went at least twice more to the police station. He told me he stood patiently talking to the officer at the front, who paged through his files, then looked up and said, why are you so worried about it, *meneer?* He looked at my husband. He was deciding, I suppose, what kind of person my husband was.

Howard relayed the conversation to me: I'm worried about it, sir, because a young woman has gone missing, yes, I am worried. I am very worried. You should be too, sir. The officer, he said, sat back in his chair. We got bigger things to worry about than that, *meneer,* big trouble all sorts of places here. We worry about keeping you people safe in your houses, *meneer,* are you safe in your house, *meneer?* I am safe, thank you, sir. That's not the point. Other people are not safe, that's what I'm worried about. And then the officer said, be grateful we keep you safe in your house, *meneer,* don't worry about the other people. You said she's a young lady, this Black? She probably ran off with someone, what d'you expect. Probably doing something she shouldn't be, what do you know about it?

Howard left in a fury. He came home and poured himself a whisky, he seldom did that. He fumed, then became silent. I went out back and told Emily there was no news about Tiny.

ONE MORNING I went back to my studio. It had the air of an abandoned place, everything just as I'd left it, weeks before. I started tidying it, then I went to the house and got a cloth, for wiping and dusting. I couldn't ask Josias or Emily to clean my studio, I didn't want them in there, I didn't want anyone in there, I've explained before.

I went to my painting, I had covered it with a sheet, it stood against the side wall. I threw the sheet off, I undraped it. It looked like an old, a very old, friend. A distant friend, an acquaintance only. Someone whose face you recognized, but distantly. I sat on my chair. I studied the painting. It had . . . how can I say . . . lost its life. It had lost its life. The light it used to hold within it was gone. Vanished. Like Tiny. Why compare it to Tiny, that was absurd. And not right. But the sense of absence, of a space where something — someone — once was, was the same.

I started going back to the studio in the mornings after that, I started fiddling with some other, smaller, canvases. That was alright, I started to relax. I fixed a small abstract, an oil, I didn't care much for it, but I finished it, it had some beauty in it. I would frame it, I thought, and give it to my mother. But then I thought she didn't really like or understand abstracts. Perhaps, then, Howard might have it for his office. I would see if Howard wanted it.

I'D BEEN ONCE to Howard's office. I had been in town for an appointment near his building, a tall dark building that shadowed the others around it. Traffic and horns blaring, I didn't like it there. Which is strange, because I love New York. Its canyons, its noise. But Johannesburg's city centre had an air of decay about it, hard to explain. Perhaps it was a residue of the colonial, the British colonial overlords, which hung and clung to its buildings like an old, sour smell. Or it was the decay, the decay that was its moral decay: the Black workers who powered Johannesburg, yet were disenfranchised. You felt it there, you felt it. Black men hung around at corners smoking cigarettes, on breaks from their jobs, or unemployed. Perhaps not many were unemployed, the job market was strong. Perhaps other people felt the excitement of the city, the jobs, the economic power of it, because it had that, certainly. You'd see, coming in, the commuter lines, thousands of Black people coming into Johannesburg to work, lines and lines of them.

Howard drove to work every day. I had driven, that day.

THIS TIME I had a dentist appointment in the city. It was a simple enough drive for me, through the winding, treed streets, to Oxford Road, soon I'd see the city's buildings up ahead, and a haze on the horizon, and then . . . into the streets, the grey streets, the traffic lights, of the city centre.

eGoli, city of gold.

Not that large a city; not a beautiful city.

I parked at a meter.

The dentist was in one of the tall buildings, it had an old stairwell with iron railings, and there was the smell of the dentist's office, so strong. The receptionist behind glass said, when will you bring the children in again, Mrs. Kline, and I stood there and scheduled the children's appointments, arranging to bring them next time.

I emerged into the bright sun on Rissik Street after my appointment and decided to go up to Howard's office a few doors down, I'd surprise him. I'd never done such a thing.

'1906' was carved into the stone on the lintel of Howard's building. A colonial city, as I said. I walked through the tall stone doorway, into the hallway, and to an old elevator with brass doors, a white man in a dark maroon uniform operating it. *Middag, mevrou,* he said. *Middag, meneer,* I said, as I stepped across the small iron gap and into the elevator. Six, please, I said, as he pressed the large button, a faded numeral six on its face, and pulled the lever, the heavy brass lever, down. I love those old elevators now, my own apartment has one. But in Johannesburg, then, they alarmed me. Perhaps I was vulnerable to a kind of claustrophobia, something like that. I would walk, I thought, not take the elevator when I was coming down. I stepped out into the dim corridor of the sixth floor, thank you sir, *dankie meneer,* I said behind me to the operator, as he moved to pull the gate shut.

And then a heavy dark door, wood. A brass nameplate:
Benator, Jones, Kline
Attorneys-at-law
I pushed it open.

Ah, Mrs. Kline, the receptionist said, at once, as she looked up and saw me, standing uncertainly at the door, the wide reception room and its soft chairs in front of me. She was a young woman, carefully dressed, I'd met her at a company Christmas party, perhaps the one just past. She stood and came right to me, so lovely to see you, she said. I smiled, thank you, Candace, it's nice to be here. I was just at the dentist's and thought I'd drop in. Oh, please, Mrs. Kline, will you have some tea? Not at all, not at all, thank you, I said. Perhaps if Howard is free? Have a seat, she said.

I sat on a low green-covered chair, the day's *Rand Daily Mail* was on the table in front of me, I remember it because that morning I had read of a mine accident, another mine accident, like the ones I've mentioned, before. There were some quiet prints on the walls, no art or paintings, an old map was one. I stood to look at it. It was an old — almost antique — map of Johannesburg, it had thin black lines, and faint cursive, I traced the lines with my eyes, to Rissik Street, where we were. And then I heard Howard's voice, I turned to see him striding down the passage, ahead of Candace, towards me.

Is everything alright, he said. Oh, yes, yes. Was just at the dentist, I said. Ah, he said. You've hardly ever been here! We laughed then, all three of us. I should give you another tour, he said. And Candace said, yes, you'll see how we spend our days. We laughed, the three of us, again.

Howard took me back down the passage, a fine rug — perhaps Persian — on the wooden floor. There were his partners' doors on each side, closed, and a small hallway, then, where a secretary sat. She was older, bespectacled, I had met her at a Christmas party too. She stood up and smiled. Please, please,

83

sit down, I said, it's lovely to see you. And you! she said. And then, to the right, we turned into Howard's office.

His office was spare, it had a filing cabinet, and a large wooden desk with a green leather blotter, worn. There was an old armchair with faded covering. Howard had a single photograph, of us, of us four. It was taken I don't know when, on holiday at the sea in Durban, we windblown and in bathing suits: me, him, the two children. The children were much smaller, they might have been eight and five years old, it was an old photo. Don't you want a new one, I said, it's old, this one. Ah, it's a nice picture, he said. It was in a dark leather frame my parents had given him, it stood, facing the room, on a shelf behind his desk.

I knew it, I said then. You need some paintings on your walls! Why didn't you say something, I have lots of small things for you. Ah, doesn't matter, he said.

His tall window, double-sashed and framed in dark wood, overlooked the south part of the city, and I stood there. To the southwest was Soweto, you could see it. It stretched, far as the eye could see, low and still from this distance, small glints in the sun here and there, from a car perhaps, or a window, or from some piece of metal.

I turned then to the bookcase. I knew Howard's books, he'd kept them at home in his study, before. When I met Howard, he was doing his law degree, his books always with him. Some of the briefs, leather-bound now, were in the bookcase. And there were old textbooks: *Roman–Dutch Law in South Africa. The Law and the Courts. British Common Law.* Others. It was a sober room. A lawyer's room, what else.

He had a lamp on his desk, a grey reading lamp, the ordinary kind you buy in a hardware store. It was on, its strong, white light fell on the pile of papers on the desk. The papers were stacked in an immaculate pile. Immaculate like Howard, I thought then.

I can find you a nice lamp, I said. I'm sure I have a nicer one at home. Howard wasn't interested in that. Never mind, he said. You can bring me a painting though, we can find one at home tonight. I liked that idea. It filled me at once with warmth. I had something to do now, something to look for in my studio.

I thought of the one I had considered for my mother. And I had many other small works, even some watercolours, I used to paint watercolours too, before I abandoned them and worked only in oil. Although, I then thought: watercolours don't go in this room, this office. No. A watercolour wouldn't be right. I would find an oil. A darker, more sombre one, of those I had.

Howard's law work was corporate, he had tried to explain it to me, but I wasn't interested. Or, I didn't understand it, not really. He worked for companies, large steel companies, and Anglo American, the mining conglomerate, was his client, I think he said that once. He didn't do political work. His colleague, though, Jack Benator, did some small work on political cases, preparing papers, he worked for advocates defending people, Black people. I knew that. It's Benator who had brought Joseph, the activist, to Howard, after all. Frederick Jones, the third partner, was in sympathy too, how could it have worked otherwise? But Jones did only corporate work, like Howard.

They were a small firm, under the radar probably, and Jack Benator could take on the work that he wanted and believed in. Howard simply kept to his clients, and didn't speak much further about it.

The black phone rang on Howard's desk. Yes? he said. Okay, okay, thank you, Candace, will be out shortly. I have a client now, Jacqueline, he said, and looked at his watch. Thanks, darling, I said, thanks for having me here again. It's quite nice, really — it is! And then I left, Howard leading me back down the passage, past the secretary who said goodbye, back to the reception room and Candace, goodbye Mrs. Kline, she said.

A man in a suit, some papers on the table in front of him, was sitting in the low, green chair. Howard pulled the heavy wooden door open, and was going to walk me to the elevator. I'm going to take the stairs, I said. Howard shook his head, silly, you know there's nothing to be afraid about an elevator. He smiled. See you later, I said, and I walked to the stairwell. EXIT, it said, in red, with a black illustration of stairs, a stick figure walking down them.

The stairs, the six flights, wound in a circular route, a polished stone floor, down and down, I could look over the heavy iron railing and see the tiled floor, a maroon-and-beige floor, below. I remember my hand on the rail. Across that old floor then on the ground floor, past a man, a Black man lounging in the doorway, and out onto Rissik Street. How bright it seemed outside. For a moment I felt sorry for Howard, closed in that sombre space, doing sombre work, his papers, papers, all day. And then I found my car, it had a parking ticket, a tell-tale white slip curled on the dash under the wiper.

I was careless with time, things like that. I hadn't thought, when I paid the meter, about the extra time, the unplanned visit to Howard's office. Twenty rand. I would give the white slip to Howard that evening. Howard would never have got a ticket and he would be irritated. For a moment I thought of hiding it, the ticket, and paying it myself. But what was the point? Howard knew me, I say that — again.

THAT AFTERNOON when I got home, I didn't rest. I went down into my studio. I pulled out old canvases, small works I had done over the years. The watercolours I put to one side. I didn't like them. I felt them to be transient, that they could melt away. I've said before: I'd stopped working in watercolour. They wouldn't work in Howard's office either, Howard's office which had an air of solidity and permanence, of age, even. (But Howard, Howard was young! He was only in his thirties then.)

I came upon, then, a group of works I had done after visiting my parents in Villiers one weekend. They were abstracts, but you could see, could feel, the Vaal River within them. Or I could see it, feel it.

A heavy, a great river. That river was filled with brown silt, I knew it so well, from swimming in it as a child. A deep sandy bottom, I remember the feel of it as my toes, my feet, sank into it. I'd almost drowned in that river once. This is true.

IT WAS MY UNCLE BERNARD who took me swimming in the river. Bernard was my father's brother, and his business partner, they ran the shop, the business, in Villiers. Bernard was much younger than my father, not yet married, then.

It must have been a Sunday afternoon, he said he'd take me down to the river in his car, he'd take me swimming. How vividly I remember the towel on my lap, as I sat in the front seat next to him. I liked him, he joked a lot, and he was more carefree than my father. I think he loved me dearly.

We drove, drove the quiet grey streets of Villiers, down the hill towards the river, which we could see then, visible through the willow trees that bowed over the banks. The river, seen like that, was a ribbon of brown, it glinted here and there in the sun. But when you got down to the river, after my uncle had parked the car and we'd got out, you saw that the river was large, and very wide. So wide. It had a current too, it wasn't peaceful. It was on its way somewhere; this sojourn in Villiers, our town, was a small stop for the river. I knew this: I'd seen its brownness — its wideness — moving across the landscape as we followed it, when my father drove us to Vrede, or Frankfort, neighbouring towns, on weekends. The river wound in a slow, large way.

I'd also seen maps of the river, at school. *Die Groot Vaal,* my teacher called it, the Great Vaal. It was woven into the history of our country, it marked the boundary between the Orange Free State and what became the Transvaal, the two provinces. It had been impassable in distant years, crossing it was haz- ardous and had surely killed people: Indigenous people, Black people, as well as Boers in ox wagons, oxen themselves, and, later, the English, English soldiers, wagons pulled under, guns and weapons swept away.

The river flooded and overran its banks, I don't know how many times a year, it was when the great rains came. A sight: the pale brown water — so much of it — rising under cars, to their windscreens, rising and flooding roadways, the grey streets of Villiers, gardens, fences, right up to the porches of houses.

And then it retreated.

But the day I went swimming with my uncle was an ordinary day, an ordinary day for the river: a hot, still, summer day.

We put our towels on the great flat rock on the bank, there were other children and young people swimming. Their parents too, and other adults, like my uncle. I remember the warmth of the sun. Perhaps I was nine years old, it seems to me I must have been nine years old.

I didn't swim much. I'd been taught to swim in the river by my father, but I'd never had lessons, the way children do now. I did some version of the dog paddle, the dog paddle they call it. I think that's what I did.

My uncle took me out, we were splashing, splashing next to the other children and teenagers. They were people from Villiers, I knew some of them, they were all Afrikaners, that's who lived in my town. We were one of the few English-speaking families in Villiers. They shouted in Afrikaans, *kom, kom, in met jou, in met you, meisie,* they shouted.

Perhaps I felt goaded, perhaps I did.

My uncle said, let's go out farther. And I followed him, treading out into the stream.

I watched the other children recede, on the rock, in the shallows. I was farther out than them. I felt a bit of pride, then. I'm not a competitive person, why did I feel that? Perhaps because I was an only child, I was always aware of my aloneness, I felt other children had brothers and sisters, and I — I wished to assert myself as someone distinct. Something like that. I don't know.

And then my uncle and I were afloat in the middle of the river. I could no longer feel the sand bottom that I knew the feel of, so well. My head was just above the surface of the water, its brownness stretched away on all sides, and I could see the pale greenness of the bank, the willows, which seemed distant, a line, merely, now.

And then the current became too strong for me. I was small, after all, my paddling was no match for the current. Uncle Bernie, I shouted. I say I shouted, but I imagine my weak, girl's voice. My uncle was floating well, he was enjoying the water. Jackie, he called. No, no, I said, and he turned to see me now, a way away from him, down the stream.

I saw his eyes, then, and I remember, even now, the look in them. My Uncle Bernard.

It was a while, a long while it seems to me, that we struggled and were carried, both of us now, down the stream. The bank with its large flat rock where we'd started was nowhere in sight. Now there was only brownness, and pale green in a wavering line along both banks. And the sun, of course the sun, its flash, which was like an attack. I remember the glinting of my uncle's dark, wet head, I kept my eyes on it.

A large rock midstream was coming up ahead and my uncle pushed himself towards me with what strength I do not know, and he got hold of my waist, my small body, and pulled us both to the rock. And then, after clinging, clinging to the rock for some minutes, he pulled us to the side, I don't know how he did it. We were out of the current. I watched the current, going without me. It went, went on, without me. Without us.

The river moved into the trees, the distant trees, and away, and I couldn't see it any more after that. It went to the sea.

All rivers go to the sea.

I'VE SAID MANY TIMES I loved that river. I love it still, and I haven't set eyes on it in forty-four years. A part of me would like to see it again before I die, but I think that I will not.

How can you love something that almost killed you? Perhaps that's the question that haunts me, with everything. Because I love South Africa, yet I came out of there in shreds. You *can* love something that wounded you. It took me a long time to understand that.

ELENA SAID TO ME recently, tell me about the time you nearly died in the river, Mom, tell me that story again. Oh Helena, I said. Do you remember how you and Stephen used to make me tell that story again and again when you were small? I'm not telling it again, I'm just not, I said.

I wish I could see that river, Mom, Helena said.

Perhaps it's changed now, I said. I don't know.

Rivers don't change, Helena said then.

BUT THERE WAS the group of paintings, the oils that came after a visit one weekend to Villiers. The paintings carried in them, unmistakably, that river. Abstracts, but they held the largeness, the brownness, of that river. Its power. That undercurrent that could take everything along with it, in its wake. My paintings, that group, had that.

I set up three of them, I think there were four or five, I'd had to dig them out. They had been stacked against each other, against the wall. I set them up, one at a time, on my easel, then I sat on my chair. They weren't large, I've said that.

They were perfect for Howard, for his office. I'd had a look at his office again, I felt satisfaction in that. I could picture exactly where they would be. But only one of them. Only one.

The paintings were variations on a theme, often I felt I was repeating myself in my work, but I know, now, that artists do that, all artists do that. I worried about it then. I thought I might not have what it took to create new things, that I would keep repeating myself, and repeating. I would run out of material, new material. Sometimes this thought — close to fear — woke me at night.

I chose one painting for Howard.

When he came home that evening I told him, as he came into our room and kissed me hello, that I had chosen a painting for his office, I was so pleased! He was pleased that I was pleased. As I said before, Howard didn't care what was on the walls of his office, he wouldn't have cared about such a thing. I understood Howard too.

And then I added, it's a surprise though. I'll have it framed and I'll bring it in a couple of weeks. Oh, I'm really happy about it, I remember saying, again. We went to the children, and in to dinner.

The next afternoon I took the canvas and drove with it to my framer. He was farther away, farther than my usual week-day route to ballet and Eric. André had been making frames for artists for a long time, Eric had suggested him originally, and he'd never led me wrong with a frame. Sometimes I doubted myself with frames, I felt they weren't part of my canvas and they were hard to match, to find a frame that didn't intrude on my own work. But André was good.

We stood together, André brought out frame after frame. I like the painting, he said. André didn't like everything I brought him, so this meant a lot. He was right in the end about the frame I think, because we disagreed over one or two, but then I saw he must be right.

I wish I could remember now what frame we chose, I have such a vivid memory of the painting, but no memory of the frame. And where that painting is now, I don't know. Perhaps Stephen took it, because it came to New York with us. Yes, perhaps Stephen took it for his first apartment, I have an idea Howard told him it had come from his office, please, take it, Howard would have said.

A WEEK LATER I picked up the framed painting and drove it to Howard's office. There was quite a scene with it then, because I was so particular about where it should hang. Candace had come from the reception into Howard's office, his own office, and was admiring the painting and giving suggestions about which wall, what height. I became very tense, the chatter between Howard and Candace so annoying, and I, anxious to have my way with the placement. I became even more anxious because I didn't want to be rude to Candace and soon I was almost in tears. Ah, Candace, call Frans from downstairs, will you, Howard said, ask him to come up with hammer and nails. I knew at once that Howard had understood how I felt, how close I was to tears. And Candace went to get Frans.

Frans, the Black man, came up with his toolbox, a battered box that rattled as he walked. André had connected the picture wire, but the nails? For a moment I thought of André, and wished I'd brought him. I was sure the Black man would do it all wrong, I had to rummage with him through his box, through the nails, nails and nails of all sizes, to find the right one, and then direct him, so carefully, to a pencil mark I'd made on the wall. And he hammered the nail in: gently, I said. Candace and Howard were silent, they were watching, now and then Candace would say, just to the left a touch, a tiny bit lower, Mrs. Kline. I remember so clearly Candace's blue skirt and white blouse, she was a slim girl, so young. It was embarrassing.

But the painting, in the end, was hung.

It was hung exactly where I wanted it, it was directly across from Howard's desk. Some light fell across it, the right amount and kind of light, from the window. We — I, Howard, Candace, and Frans — stood together, stepped back, and looked at it. We stood in silence, we stood. Then Frans said, ah, okay *baas,* is done then. As if from a trance Howard turned and said, yes, it's done, thanks, Frans. Thank you. And Candace said, stirring, it's the perfect spot, Mrs. Kline, you were right, look how the sun falls on it. Her voice was softer than it usually was, and she looked again at the painting. It's very beautiful, she said. Thank you, Candace, I said, and I turned and hugged her. I don't know what came over me, I never hug people.

YOU'VE ASKED ABOUT my children, how they were. They were happy children. Helena liked reading, as I did. She continued with her ballet classes, she became better and better. She spent hours at home prancing around on the tiles, practising her pirouettes. She'd have me watch, then she'd have Emily watch. She'd trip sometimes over Emily's cleaning buckets, her vacuum. I'd hear Josias admonish her: Helena, don't jump where I'm busy, don't jump!

The dogs would follow Helena around when she danced. There'd be barking then. Chester, especially, was playful that way. The other dog, Teddy, was an Alsatian, he'd been a neighbour's dog and they had moved to Cape Town. We offered to take him, we'd been thinking of getting another dog for the children. But Teddy was old, perhaps it had been a mistake to take him. He was frail, often I had to take him to the vet. He was like a grandfather, or an old lion, perhaps the children enjoyed that. They'd joke about him, about his age, his grumpiness. He didn't play or respond much to them and their teasing. He stuck close to Chester though: where Chester went, he was never far behind. He lay around, and slept, I'd see him sleeping under the laundry lines, in the yard.

When we went to Villiers to visit my parents, Helena would disappear for hours, later I discovered where she went. A room at the back of my parents' house had a cupboard you could walk into, you could shut the door behind you. There was even a light, it was an enchanted cupboard, for a child. The cupboard was filled, floor to ceiling, with books, old books. They were the books of my childhood. *What Katy Did,* followed by *What Katy Did at School* and *What Katy Did Next,* and others

I don't remember. Books about girls that I wished I could be, or about girls living lives quite unlike mine. Where, in those girls, was I?

Occasionally I see copies of those books, antiquarian books now, there's a store on 59th Street where I once saw the *What Katy Did* series, it was behind glass in a heavy wooden bookcase. The books had dark red covers, faded, and it was so dim in there, behind that old glass, in that sanctum. I thought I would not disturb the books there, in their dark resting place, that case, it seemed wrong to take them, I would not take them, no.

But my childhood was filled with those books, I'd be reading, reading, I'd lie on a blanket outside. I had a wool blanket, I remember its roughness. I'd drag it out onto the grass, with my book.

Or I'd have with me a sketch pad and pencil.

When I was small I was always scribbling with one of those old yellow pencils I carried around. I'd scribble on any scrap of paper, or discarded label, or the newspaper. And then I'd keep the scraps in the pockets of a cotton dress I was wearing, or in a drawer in my room. I was trying to write something; or draw something. My mother bought me a sketch pad finally, as the torn-up pieces of paper all over the house annoyed her. The sketch pad wasn't large, and it became my habit to hide it: under my bed, or in a drawer, or under a chair in the living room. If I carried it around I'd hold it close to me, wrapped in a cardigan. Why did I do that? I always did that. I felt the wish to draw as a subversive thing, and secret.

AS I LAY on the grass, there'd be no sound, a buzz of cicadas, that's all. The hot sun. A cotton dress. My bare feet.

One of my dresses was white with tiny blue flowers. Cornflowers. I'd never seen real cornflowers, they didn't grow naturally in South Africa.

My books, too, were filled with things I'd never seen. Snow. White Christmases. English muffins. Boarding schools. Green, green fields, and mist. I had an idea those things were in the real world, and where we were was a lesser, less important, less impressive world. It took me years to understand and recognize that this outpost of veld was beautiful, too.

I'd have a snack with me on the blanket: a peach, or an apple.

And sometimes as I lay there through the long afternoons my mother would come out, she had a rose garden. She'd had a Black man from my father's shop come to dig it out for her once. Over here, over here, she'd said to him. Careful, careful now! Not too much, just this size is fine. Careful, boy! Yes ma'am, yes ma'am, he said, and he pushed his spade into the earth, and stood, leaning on it, for a moment. And then he'd carried on. I remember his spade, his tattered shirt, his thin legs. The earth wasn't dark and rich, it was pale and hard and cracked, it must have been a challenge to make a rose garden there.

My mother and the Black man spent an afternoon creating a space for the roses. The Black man said nothing, just yes ma'am, yes ma'am, once every while, as she stood there, on the grass in her low heels, her stockings, her small-patterned dress, there were her pale hands.

Soon enough my mother became irritated, ah, let's leave

it now, just leave it. Leave the spade, just leave it, she said. Yes ma'am, he said.

My mother walked carefully across the grass. What are you doing, Jacqueline, she said as she passed me. Reading, Mom, just reading, I said. Careful the sun, she said, don't burn, Jacqueline.

I watched her walk in her careful way up the red stone stairs, into the house. I watched her pale stockinged legs. I wondered if I'd have to wear stockings like that one day.

I've never worn stockings.

The Black man looked across the grass at me, then he walked, a slow walk, wiping his hands on his shorts, around the back, I heard the creak of the back gate, the rusted metal, he must've gone into our yard, the grey yard where Maggie's room was, near the washing lines.

Perhaps Maggie made him tea, in one of her dark tin mugs. Perhaps she gave him a slab of white bread and her jam, that she'd spoon from its tin, its large tin. Smooth Apricot Jam, it said on the outside. A deep orange.

Perhaps the man sat on her wooden chair, under the eave, away from the sun, so hot, then. I imagine they spoke a little. About the madam and what the madam wants, ah, that madam. A click of the man's tongue. And then a conversation in their language about something else, about what was going on these days, at the Location. Maggie wouldn't have been there for a while. The Location: that place I'd seen from my father's car, sprawling, tin glinting a little in the flat sun. Along the long, straight road. Nothing, nothing else, there.

But the garden, the rose garden, was made. My mother spent so many hours with her roses, I remember her standing, her low heels as she walked on the grass, the prickly grass, and the small gardening gloves she put on, then.

I paid little attention to the roses, but I have an idea there were different kinds, different strains. I'd see her supervising, again, that Black man, as he brought boxes filled with pots, to plant. I'd see her arguing with him as they stood, a click of his tongue, again. Like this, she'd say. Like this. And she'd point. And they'd carry on: a strange partnership, surely.

There were peach-coloured roses, and pale pink ones, many were pale, pale blooms turned this way, or that, like small, frail people.

Under the sun, my mother's roses flourished. How did they flourish, in that dry soil, under that bright, unwavering sun? I thought of their thorns, a shape unmistakable: small, sharp talons.

My mother never picked the roses, or brought them into our house. She didn't arrange them in a vase or anything like that. Here I see roses everywhere, in flower shops, red roses, a dozen at a time, sometimes they're tightly budded, and sometimes open and luxuriant. And white roses, even white roses. I've been in people's homes with crystal vases filled, filled with roses, so many roses. I don't like them.

Once here Stephen and his wife Marie arrived at our apartment, an occasion I don't remember, but it was winter, and snow, snowflakes on Stephen's dark coat, he shaking them off, and the stamping of feet at the door, on the mat, laughing. Boots off, and then Stephen: what weather! More exclamations and then Marie, her cheek cool, chilled from outside, I remember kissing her, and she was bearing flowers: a dozen white roses. The flowers were swathed in their tissue paper, and I took them, they had almost no weight, just that paper, rustling, or breathing, I opened them, and their scent, their white scent, and their pallor, came at once at me, and I felt ill and had to give them to Howard. And then Marie said, come, let's find a vase, but I pretended to be fiddling with something else while Marie went into the kitchen, cupboards opening and closing, and then she emerged with a glass vase, and more fussing in the kitchen, cutting, she had found a scissors.

Perhaps Howard later told Stephen that I had an allergy to some flowers, or he made some other excuse, I don't know.

Howard never bought me roses.

BUT THERE WERE those long afternoons in Villiers when I was a girl. As I lay outside on my blanket reading, I'd sometimes hear the voices of children, teenagers calling and whooping on the wide street. They'd be on their bicycles. And then I'd sit up, and watch them, their wheeling, wheeling down the street. Bare feet, their feet so fleet on the pedals. I never learned to ride a bicycle.

I'd feel my aloneness, then. I knew some of the children, they were from my school, the only school in our town, but they were Afrikaners, Afrikaans. I'd hear their language, and sometimes they'd call to me, *meisie, meisie, daar's sy, daar's sy*, and they'd laugh or whoop, and wheel again, perhaps showing off. I envied them their ease, their slow swoops down the street. I, behind my iron garden gate, the roses, my mother's roses by, the pale rocks with their slow, black lizards behind me, against the house's wall.

THE SUMMER MONTHS of 1972 started turning, turning to autumn. It was April.

Autumn wasn't beautiful in Johannesburg, the leaves don't turn the way they do here, we didn't care much for autumn. Josias started cleaning up the pool in preparation for winter, the pool simply lay for the few winter months under a grey tarpaulin, and its water became green, green with algae, under it. Josias's work with Howard and the chlorine would stop, and now there was one less thing for Josias to do, one less thing for Howard to share with him.

Joseph was still in our garden room. It had been more than three months. I'd say to Howard, Howard, really, when is this going to end. It's not right. He'll be found one day and then what? He's made it this far, Howard would say, I don't think he'll be found. It's fine. What's it to you, Jacqueline, he'd say. I became angry then. It's my space, I said. What are you talking about, it's not your space, you can't see or hear him from your studio, you're just being ridiculous. Our conversations went like that.

Once I told Howard, well, I have to order more food you know, his milk, bread, tea. Our leftovers. Emily has to go down there twice a day, she resents it. This, this, was a lie. I'd seldom lied before. I'm sure I'd seldom lied.

Howard laughed abruptly then. We're not short of money, Jacqueline, order him whatever food you want, you know that.

I knew that, of course I knew that. I didn't try that argument again. I could hear the falseness in my voice, my soft voice that I came to hate.

And then later, reading in bed under the lamp, I'd be disturbed by my thoughts. What does Benator say, for God's sake, I'd say. It's Jack who brought him here, isn't he going to take some responsibility? Howard looked at me and shook his head. He didn't answer.

Once, after I'd been on about Jack Benator again, he said, look, alright Jacqueline, I'll ask Jack what's going on. I'll ask him if Joseph can be moved. Okay?

For a brief time, I felt hopeful.

BUT HOWARD SPOKE TO JACK, who said these were bad times, people were being picked up every day. Jack said Joseph's colleagues were very grateful, our home had been remarkably intact as a harbour.

I should hope so, I said. But what if he is found, found out, I said. Then we are compromised.

Howard looked at me. How was he not afraid? Howard, with his mild nature, his wish to help people, was naïve. I had never thought that before.

Aren't you worried? I said. I'm not worried, Jacqueline, I'm just not worried. The police will never come here, they don't come snooping around yards in Illovo: they're looking for minor things here, pass offences, that's all. Most of the activists they're looking for are Black, they're in Soweto.

Howard, I said, come on.

Howard was wrong, he was wrong.

Was this simply blindness, what was it?

You know they're looking for the students, the intellectuals, the lawyers, the whites as well, come on, Howard.

Yes, Howard said, but not in a corporate lawyer's house in Illovo, they're just not. They haven't found him yet, have they? he said.

I had no answer for that.

But I was alarmed, alarmed at what I felt was Howard's blindness, his naïveté. And what about Jack Benator, I said. They could figure something out with him, and that leads straight to you.

Then I tried something different. The children, Howard. How can you not think of the children? Seriously, what if he is found and you and I are compromised?

Jacqueline, I'm tired of this now. I'm going to bed, he'd say.

I didn't sleep.

AND THEN the weather turned. Not a sharp turn, the seasons don't turn so sharply there, I've said that before, but that year — that year — I remember summer ending.

I had Josias bring out an old bar heater from the garage and carry it down to the garden room. I said, just leave it out-side at the door, Josias, I'll take care of it. And then I thought, I have a real reason, an excuse now, I will go and talk to Joseph.

I had been going into my studio every day, but I've not mentioned it, because those visits now became visits of pain. The painting stood, a vacancy, and I, my helpless, spattered hands, looking at it. I've said before: I'd sit in my chair, and look at it again. How many times can one look at a painting, and fail to see its light, fail to see what it needed? I felt such a sense of failure, I felt so useless.

What if I lost my painting for good, what if I was unable to paint again at all?

I'd fiddle with other small canvases then, I'd fix something small on one, then I'd spend days moving things around in the studio, believing I was tidying it. I cleaned my tubes, threw old ones out, sometimes I just sat in the chair, my head against its wood back, and closed my eyes. That helped. Peace would come, my mind would settle. A temporary reprieve.

But I would go and see Joseph in the garden room.

I LEFT, ONE DAY, my studio at noon, and walked under the dim trees, across to the garden room. The heater Josias had brought was next to the door. I went to the door, that door that now inhabited my dreams, and knocked. It was such a thin knock in the silence of the garden, a glade, it was. I heard the knock, so small, like a child's. And I felt like a child. A timid, frightened child.

I heard the scrape of a chair, something like that, inside, and, instantly, the door opened, and he was there, standing there, and he saw me. Me. It was me.

Jacqueline, he said. How nice to see you. Is everything alright? He looked into my face. Oh yes, yes, everything's fine, I said. I think my voice was small, tight in my throat. Come in, come in, Jacqueline, he said, and he opened his door, and stepped aside, and gestured me in.

All those months, four months, and I'd not seen him, or come into his room.

I'd imagined it, how I'd imagined it, that space. There were more books than I'd imagined, a pile, many high. More papers, many papers, but in an orderly pile on the table, and several other piles, all over the room, some on the concrete floor. A briefcase, next to his table. My table, an old table I'd hauled from the garage. His chair, my chair, a wooden chair, pushed back, he must've been sitting in it, right before.

And his bed. A narrow bed, like a prisoner's. Or like Josias's bed, I'd seen Josias's, in his small concrete room. But Joseph's bed was neatly made. Immaculate. The white sheets I'd put there, the pillow, the wool blanket, blue. And a chill in the room, the weather had turned, as I said.

In the corner, some of our white dishes, two or three, and a cup, were stacked — dirty dishes, Emily would pick them up that afternoon, I knew. And next to them, on the floor, plugged into the outlet, was our old kettle, its dusty, worn silver that I remembered. And there was the small, white fridge.

That's all there was. I think that's all.

The lone light bulb on the ceiling cast a thin, yellow light, and filtered sunlight came through the two small windows, as I'd imagined, so many times. The windows, I saw now, were not clean (how could they be clean?), they needed washing. More light would come then, more light. I thought I would ask Josias to wash them, inside and out. No, Emily. Josias mustn't come in here, I remembered. Josias had never been in here.

Before I stepped in I said, Joseph, I'm here to bring you a heater, it's winter soon, it must be cold in here. I had to give him a reason for my being there.

I turned and gestured outside to the heater. This is wonderful, he said. Thank you. And then he moved outside, and bent down, lifting the heater with both hands, it wasn't heavy, a small portable thing it was, and carried it over the threshold, past me, into the room.

I stepped in. I didn't close the door behind me, that felt wrong. Jacqueline, he said, I must close the door. There's no one down here, I said. I know, he said. But I must. And he walked past me and pushed the door shut. It scraped on its frame as he pushed.

And then we were together in that small space. So still. I looked at him, looked at him properly, then.

He looked more groomed than I imagined. His dark beard was thick but trimmed, and his hair was not long, it must have been recently cut. By whom? I thought then of his nights, those many nights, with colleagues in Soweto, in other safe houses, and the help, the support he got. Someone to cut his hair. Suddenly, I wanted to cut his hair.

His glasses were clean, his eyes dark behind them. I'm so sorry for all this, Jacqueline, he said. So sorry. I'm so grateful to you and Howard. Our work is proceeding. We work on, you know. I know, I said. I couldn't think what else to say. We'd better plug your heater in, I said.

He carried the heater to the plug where the kettle and fridge were, the only outlet in the room, and I said, you'll just have to unplug the kettle when the heater's on, and he laughed. Of course, it's no problem, he said. He plugged it in and right away there was the smell of burning dust, so long unused, that heater.

D'you have enough to eat, I said. Emily can bring you anything you want, you know, you have simply to ask her. I know, he said. I'm fine. I eat very well at night, my friends feed me. They know they must feed me, I'm very important to them, he said, and he laughed. I felt terrible then. I felt close to tears.

He turned away, he was quite amused by what he'd said. His frame was so thin, thinner perhaps than before, his long dark pants, his leather belt, his white buttoned shirt. And I see it now, the shirt unbuttoned at his neck, his pale throat. A pallor, no doubt about it: a pallor. I would lay my head on that white shirt, that shoulder, his thin frame beneath it. I imagined it. I felt a stab of anguish. I must go now, I said, and I turned to the door, pulled it open, and left. So quickly, so gracelessly, I see it now.

THAT AFTERNOON I told Emily that Joseph was getting thin, too thin. Take him more food, Emily, just take more things. What else can you take? Emily looked at me. Ah, ma'am. Okay. Boil some eggs every day, I said. And some apples? Take him fruit also, I said. You must ask him every time, I said, ask him what he needs. He won't ask you, he's a very polite man. That is true, ma'am, he's polite a man, a good man, is true. Emily said this as a pronouncement, or to herself, she had turned back to her work when she said it. Emily, who knew good from evil. My anguish, again, was profound.

I told Emily to wash his windows, take a bucket down there and wipe them down. I can't ask Josias to do it, I said. Emily looked at me. Josias knows about everything, she said, but okay, ma'am.

The next afternoon I watched her from my bedroom, her figure, her familiar figure, making its way down the grass, carrying a bucket, some rags under her arm. The bucket must have been full of water because she walked carefully, as though she might stumble and fall. That wasn't a job for her, I thought.

My mornings in the studio continued in the stasis, my studio started to feel unused, an abandoned shed, with me its caretaker, merely.

JOSEPH HAD TOLD ME his work was proceeding, how I remembered that word, it stuck in my mind and kept returning to me. His work was proceeding, while my work wasn't. I started reading the newspapers with more attention.

At breakfast, with the newspaper, I would scan and scan, until I found something, something I was looking for: a small explosion on the main road to Sasolburg, one day. Sabotage. I'd carry an image of that road, I'd been on it, it was the main road to the Free State, a long straight road, power lines, some shanties you could see in the distance, glinting, a lone Black man, walking.

And another day: a problem, again a small explosion, outside a police station in Ermelo, I'd been there too. A dusty town, with nothing, its police station a small squat building on the main road, manned with an officer, brutal in his language, I imagined it. I knew that language, I knew it. *Opstaan jou moer, opstaan.*

My mornings at breakfast now lost their peace. As I sat with my tea, I came to feel that the newspapers were, how can I say, my friends. They held what was true. It seemed to me if I read closely enough, I would find the truth of where we were, what was happening. I began to eat less. I told Emily I only wanted dry toast now, and sometimes I'd only have a few bites of that. Howard said I looked thin.

One morning I read, in a corner buried on page seven, of an explosion on the South Rand, near the foreman's building, not far from the mine itself. I worried, then, about the miners, the Black miners. What if they were inadvertently killed? I started to worry about many small things like that,

that filled my days, my days that I floated through, in all other ways, as before.

Did Joseph read the newspapers? He didn't have newspapers. But Joseph didn't need newspapers. Joseph and his comrades were the ones creating the news, the stories, that I was reading.

And then the mines started to fill my dreams. Their black tunnels, their raging heat, a black face, gleaming with sweat; the miner's lamplight. The clanging of iron buckets, the rails. The elevator that moved up and down, ceaselessly. A roar of dynamite, above. I'd wake, with a start.

And one day in the newspaper: an incident at a power station on the Vaal dam. Sabotage. I'd seen that power station too, from the car as we drove to Villiers. A vast complex thing, it powered Johannesburg, from that great brown river that I knew and feared. It was some kind of explosion, and a man was injured this time. A labourer, a Black man. I read that — that last — in anguish.

This was going nowhere, I thought. And then I worried about that: that the work, Joseph's work — the resistance — was all in vain. All this danger, all these attacks, would come to nothing. Nothing. Stasis, more stasis.

Howard was busy at work, his practice was growing all the time. He was preoccupied and tired when he came home, so I never told him about my fears, my new fears. He said again that I looked thin, was I alright? Fine, I said, just busy, busy with the painting. The painting is bothering me, I said.

This, as you see, was only partly true.

I DIDN'T GO to the garden room again to see Joseph. I had no
excuse, no reason, I thought. It had become cold then and
I'd think about the flimsy heater in the stone room. I'd think
of the sharp mornings, white frost on the grass. I imagined
the red element of the heater, scorching hot if you went too
close. I worried it would burn out, just die, but then I worried
it would malfunction and cause a fire. There were accidents
with heaters like that.

One night I dreamed of a vast conflagration, an explosion
of raging flames, and destruction, destruction, in its wake.
I woke with the taste of ashes, ash, in my mouth.

I hoped Joseph had warmer clothes, I worried about it.
I asked Emily to make sure, to ask him. I gave her another
blanket for his bed, a thick wool one, I said, just give it to
him, Emily, even if he says he doesn't want it. Emily nodded,
and later I watched her walk carefully down the grass with
the folded blanket, the winter grass yellow now. Emily herself in a beige cardigan. I'd given her that cardigan, an old
one of mine, and it strained, strained, against her shoulders
and rounded arms, against her back, I watched as she walked.
Perhaps I should buy Emily her own cardigan, one that fits
her, I thought then.

And Emily told me, yes ma'am, he has a sweater, he's always
in his navy sweater now. He wears a wool cap also, she said.
This was a new image for me to carry, in my mind.

And one day as Emily and I stood in the kitchen, I making
a list for the grocery order (more, more cheese, because of
Joseph), Emily told me Joseph had seen his wife. He told you?
I said. Yes ma'am, he told me his comrades make places where

he can meet his wife, they take him. This is very good, ma'am, she said, is very good. She nodded emphatically. That is wonderful, Emily, I said, that is wonderful.

But then, under my ordinary words: an odd feeling. Joseph belonged not only to me, to Emily, to us, to our garden, then. His comrades, yes, he belonged to them. But to his wife? I tried to imagine her. I could not.

I spent several days trying to conjure an image of his wife in my mind. Was she tall or short, dark-haired or fair? And then: her plight. Her husband fled: a fugitive in his own country. A vanished man. This, this was truly unimaginable.

There was Joseph's mother-in-law, I'd heard about her from the beginning. It was a house of females, then. Holding the fort. And wiretapped, their phones wiretapped, I knew that for sure, I knew about that happening. And followed by unmarked cars, wherever they went. On the other hand, Howard had said perhaps the police didn't know much about him and his work in the first place. How difficult — and dangerous — it must have been for his wife to meet with him.

But these thoughts were too much, far too much, for me. I had too many fears already. Somehow I had to stop thinking — worrying — about his wife, his children.

And my obsession, what came to be an obsession now, were the newspaper reports, small and camouflaged as I knew they were.

I kept my own informal tally: at a smaller mine, on West Reef, an explosion again, no one injured, but steel machinery damaged, the operations were reported closed for several days. Sabotage.

I'd imagine, then, the comrades in their smoky room that night, their flashing smiles. Victory. I wished I could talk to Joseph then. Howard, Howard was busy at work, and to him I said nothing.

WE ALL HAD COLDS that winter. One after the other, the children, then Howard, who never got sick, then me. Josias started coughing too, I'd hear him at the back of the kitchen, or in the yard, a hacking cough. Sidney came, Sidney was called each time, Sidney with his bag, his thermometer, his soothing voice. Sidney examined Josias in the kitchen, Josias sitting on the kitchen chair, I and the children watching. I'd never seen Josias sick.

Only Emily didn't get sick. Emily was strong.

One day though she came and told me Joseph was sick, he took a long time coming to the door this morning, he's coughing, he said he doesn't feel well, she said. I gave her a bottle of aspirin and told her to make him a large pot of tea, honey and lemon, I told her to go a few times a day, not only twice, her usual visits. I told her to ask him about a doctor, what to do about seeing a doctor. This was a new problem.

That night I told Howard. We could ask Sidney to come and have a look at him, he said. Are you crazy, I said. I don't trust Sidney. We can't take Sidney down to that room, I said. I had an image in my mind: Sidney, his trousers and buttoned shirt, his balding head, his black doctor's bag, walking unsteadily down the dry winter grass, to that room. The heater with its glowering red bar in the corner against the wall, next to the kettle, and the small, white fridge. What would Sidney think?

It was out of the question.

We worried about this for several days, as I urged Emily to keep taking Joseph lemons for his tea, then soup, the same broth she had made for all of us. I had watched her in the kitchen over her huge pot, filled with beef bones, carrots, celery. The pot simmered for hours as Emily tended it, stirred it, then the beef bones were lifted out onto a plate: giant bones, steaming. And I — I scooped the silky marrow from the bones, and spread it, warm, on thick slices of white bread. I ate it.

A life-giving soup. I felt myself revive, become stronger. I saw I'd need strength.

What I didn't see was just how much strength I needed.

EMILY SAID Joseph wasn't getting better. He likes that soup, ma'am, she said, ah, everyone likes that soup, but he's not getting better, ma'am. He needs a doctor, Sidney must come, she said.

Sharply — more sharply than I intended — I said, Sidney can't see him, Sidney doesn't know he's there, did you forget? Forget about Sidney, we'll make another plan, I said.

That night Howard said, what if we bring Joseph up here into the house, and have Sidney see him here, not in the garden room? We'll say he's a friend visiting.

I felt the familiar, new irritation with Howard. His naïveté. Bringing Joseph into the house, right into our house, from his hidden place, felt . . . wrong. And the children. It was enough the children knew a man was living in the garden room, a friend, but a secret, because of the government. Bringing him into our house? And I've said before: I didn't trust Sidney.

We'd have to introduce Joseph by name, we'd have to make up a name, Sidney would ask where he came from, who knows what Sidney would ask, I said. No. We would not do that.

Howard threw up his hands, I'm finished with this, he said.

I told you long ago this was going on too long. You could have foreseen this, I said.

THE NEXT DAY I walked myself to the garden room, in the early afternoon. I knocked, and it's true, as Emily said, he took longer to answer. And when he came to the door I could see he'd been sleeping, he was in his clothes, his wool sweater, the cap, the woolen cap, that I'd not yet seen, on his head. He was putting on his glasses. And then, when he spoke I could hear he had a cold, the cold that had come for us all.

Joseph, I said. A doctor. You need a doctor. Yes I do, he said. The comrades are bringing one, they're waiting for one they can bring. A secure person for us. Are you sure, I said. When will he come? As soon as they can get him here, they'll bring him with them one night, he said. I felt a wave of irritation then, irritation with him, all this energy I had to spend on him, on this situation.

And I said — sharply — alright Joseph, I hope so. Emily's bringing you soup and tea she says? Yes, all good and appreciated, thank you, he said. Goodbye now, I said, I hope you get better soon. And I walked away from the low door, more briskly, and sooner, than I'd planned.

I walked up the hill, the dry grass, under the weak winter sun, I strode, I feel I strode. I went straight to my bedroom and lay down and did not come out before I heard Emily ringing the bell for dinner.

HELENA CAME INTO TOWN from Vermont a few weeks ago, she spent the weekend with me. She'd been worried about me, but she had a new thing to be worried about: I was coming down with the flu, and I always decline in the winter.

She went out while I rested on Saturday, and said she'd buy food and make dinner.

My bed in New York is in a room with little natural light, it overlooks the black outside stairwell, and the old yellow wall of the next-door building, but it's a curved room, being on a corner, its one wall curves around to meet the two walls on each side. I can hear a low traffic sound, the deep hum of the city, a siren sometimes, and the creak of the old elevator, the metallic sound as its door opens or closes. Those are my neighbours, coming in or leaving. That's all.

My dresser, an old dark wood, has deep drawers laden with my things. I wear very few of them, but there are sweaters and sweaters, old ones, some folded shirts. A large, wood-framed mirror above. My face, every day, in the mirror, wan. I smooth my hair, I see myself smoothing it now, as I'm speaking.

And my bed. My bed feels so large now that I occupy it alone, although I still sleep on the window side, as I did when Howard was here, next to me. Its dark-coloured sheets and my high, thick pillows, I read propped against them, an old lamp on the night-table alongside. I have a woman who cleans my apartment once a week, she does things I find difficult now: she changes my bed linens, she vacuums. She's started taking my small basket of laundry down the elevator to the laundry room too, to the washers and dryers she operates with my card. For years I did those things myself. I never wanted to replicate my relationship with Emily, who cleaned my home, or with Josias, who did everything else. Howard never complained, he wouldn't have noticed either way. It felt . . . right, to make this small statement. To myself, who else would care. An empty statement I know, I knew even then. But my statement.

I GOT UP LATER in the afternoon and got ready for Helena's return. I wondered where she'd been, so many hours away. Perhaps she'd gone to the museum, there was an exhibition of Kerry James Marshall on, a major one, I'd told her about it, although I hadn't seen it. And then she was home, I heard the key in the lock, that old lock.

She stood in the narrow hallway, under the light, the dark come so early now. Her cheeks were flushed from the cold, her hat low over her eyes, she was brushing snow off her coat, stamping her boots on the mat. And laden with paper bags, groceries. She'd been to the greengrocer at the corner. Oh mom, she said. I saw Kerry James Marshall too. Incredible. You must go. I was pleased, pleased she had done something for herself, not just come to check up on me, cook for me.

And she cooked, she cooked dinner in the narrow kitchen, an ancient kitchen, I've never bothered to fix it up. Sometimes that annoyed Howard, Jacqueline, he'd say, get someone in to redesign it, you can have a better kitchen you know. I knew, other people had said that too, but I had no interest in another kitchen. And Helena, even Helena who loved to cook, would manage with it just fine.

I've got a new thing, she said. A bone broth, I'm going to make you a bone broth, and leave it with you in jars, then you can have some every day, until I come next. She'd bought a dozen glass jars, the old-fashioned kind with screw-top lids, she went to pick them up later, she couldn't carry it all, before.

I saw how much she enjoyed all this, and I was happy. But later as I stood watching her make the broth, I remembered . . . I remembered Emily, Emily and her soup, the gruel she made for us all when we were sick. For Joseph. Even for Joseph.

Standing in the narrow doorway I watched Helena chopping onions, then carrots, celery, there were other vegetables: she'd bought it all. She filled my largest pot, a giant stock pot, with water, and then, from the last paper bag, she took out a clear bag of bones. Large animal — beef — bones. Six, seven of them. And finally, two large chicken legs, or perhaps they were turkey legs, they were so large. She'd been to the butcher. I was alarmed at first, I don't like so much meat, sometimes meat makes me afraid. And what would I do with all that broth? It would be too much. I didn't say this, I didn't want to offend Helena. She put spices into the pot, she looked through my cupboard, filled with old spices I was sure were out-of-date and dead, but Helena found the peppercorns, the coriander seeds. You can put anything in this broth, Mom. Parsley, she said. She measured two tablespoons of apple cider vinegar from the bottle she had bought, and turned the stove on.

She talked about her son Nicholas, about him at university and about other things, as I watched the pot, the water, start to boil. I could see the large bones, I imagined their deep cavities, marrowed.

W
A
N

And then I remembered Emily, and the marrow bones at our house in Johannesburg, and the broth, the life-giving broth she had fed us.

I had not taught Emily to make that broth, where had she learned?

Helena's broth simmered for twenty-four hours in my apartment in New York. The smell, so rich and deep and many-faceted, permeated every room. It smelled of everything, you couldn't say what it smelled of. It smelled of every deep-marrowed thing. And I thought of Emily, and the winter of 1972, when we were all so sick. Including Joseph, who got sick too.

And then I said to Helena, d'you remember 1972 in Johannesburg, do you remember, Helena? Oh, she said. Yeah. I guess so. Joseph Weiss was staying with us. We called him 'the man in the room,' she said. It's not funny though, she said. No, I said. It isn't. We were silent then. Mom, let's go sit in the living room, she said, she didn't need to be standing over the pot any more.

Helena was looking at me as we sat then in the deep chairs of my living room, me — an old woman — I suddenly saw myself through her eyes.

HELENA LEFT after her visit that weekend, she left me with a pot in my fridge, of the bone broth — marrow soup, I called it. She also left several jars of it in my freezer. We had both stood in the kitchen and sucked the bones dry, spooning the deep marrow from them. I've never seen you eat that, Mom, she said. I didn't remind her about Emily, I didn't trust myself to talk about that.

123

THE WINTER OF 1972 continued, we ate Emily's soup, I ate the fragments of marrow, scooped onto slices of white bread where they melted, the rich fat soaking through onto my fingers. Perhaps we would all make it through, perhaps we would. That's what I thought.

A doctor working for the underground was finally brought one night by the comrades, to Joseph's room. He diagnosed pneumonia, prescribed antibiotics, and then Joseph recovered, at last. Emily told me, and Joseph himself told me two weeks later, when I finally went to see him again.

I'd felt I must make amends, amends for my coldness.

I imagined Joseph's life split into two separate halves: there was his daytime, in the cold stone room, in solitude, but for a twice-daily delivery of food by Emily. Bread, eggs, milk, tea. Soup. The silence of the trees that hid him.

And the white woman of the house: a cold woman. Me. I saw myself: my aloofness. I prefer to call it reticence, but what does it matter, anymore?

And then there was Joseph's life in the dark, night hours: a knock on his door, soft in the stillness and blackness outside. A comrade, a tall man, another white man: let's go, man, you ready? And Joseph, stepping out, pulling his wooden door — my door, that I knew so well — shut behind him, and following the man, walking briskly up the dark grass. Two shadows. Past the pool, glittering black. Past the patio and the table where I'd be, for breakfast. Along the side of the house against the tall white wall. Opening the yard gate, into the concrete yard where the dogs were. The dogs: a bark, but then, wagging. The dogs knew them now. Hey, Chester, Joseph would say, Chester! Past the silent washing lines, the servants' rooms dark and still on their left. And now, the back gate: unlatched. Through the gate. Pulling it shut, its latch clicking behind them. A few minutes' walking along the empty quiet street, past other white walls, other hedges and deep trees: my neighbours' houses.

And their car: a driver in it, another white man, the engine purring to life as they got in and pulled the doors shut.

And then: a silent journey in the car along the street, through other streets, circling, to Corlett Drive. Some tense words as they passed some parked cars. Then, past them. And a small, wry joke.

A traffic light. A slow traffic light. Another. And another. Out of the suburbs soon and on the main road, then the highway's yellow lights. And soon enough, the lights of Johannesburg behind them. Joseph turning around to see, because he would feel free then, perhaps free. Some kind of freedom, at least.

To Soweto, into Soweto: its houses and houses, low and dim, lit with paraffin lamps in small windows, the rutted roads, narrow, the smell of coalfires. Joseph felt more at home there than he did anywhere. I see that, I understand that, now.

The car would draw up to a house, parking along the rutted road, its engine turning off. Silence. The bark of a dog.

And then: a low doorway, a small room, well-lit, smoke-filled. Exclamations of welcome, handshakes. Some joking, then. How you get here, man? It's alright your place still? It's alright, it's alright, Joseph would say, his glasses glinting as he turned. A smile.

Then: hot curry in a styrofoam box, its meat, meat at last, its soaked white rice. Joseph eating, eating as he listened, listened. Or a plate of stew carried in from the neighbour's house. The scrape of a spoon against a metal plate. Some talk about small things; more jokes. A smoke, then; drawing that smoke into his lungs. Joseph was not usually a smoker. A beer.

And finally: to work. The charts, the papers pulled out. Maps of things: of power stations. Of mines.

To bomb the whole thing, the whole system, to the ground, the whole fucking thing. Bring it down, bring it burning down.

I felt the fury of those nights. I was with them. I lay awake in my bed next to Howard and urged them on, in my mind.

Bring the fucking thing down.

Howard slept.

BUT I MENTIONED amends. I felt I must make amends for my coldness. I went down that day and knocked on Joseph's door. Again, right away he opened the door, and was in the doorway. Jacqueline, he said, come in. And I stepped in. I'm so sorry, Joseph, I said, we've had a bad winter, all of us sick. I'm so glad you're better, I said. And I smiled. He was still wearing his navy sweater, and a white collar I saw beneath it, at his neck. His beard was groomed, still groomed. His hair, groomed too.

Does someone cut your hair, Joseph, I said. It was such a strange thing to say, I felt embarrassed at once. Why had I said that, where did it come from? I hadn't planned to say it. He looked astonished, then he laughed. He really laughed. And I laughed too.

But really, I said. I'm curious.

He looked at me. There's a woman at the house where we go at night, she sits me in a chair, she covers my shoulders with a white sheet, she takes out her scissors, she cuts my hair. I shook my head, we both smiled, in disbelief and amazement. She's employed at a hairdresser in town, he said. She told me, you have to look reasonable, Joseph, you have to stay reasonable.

Reasonable, I said. We laughed again. Have a seat, Jacqueline, he said.

No, I said. I have something I want to give you. I looked around the room, I had looked around it before, but this time I was looking at its walls, its whitewashed, faded walls.

I'm going to bring you a painting, I said.

He was silent. I think he was moved. He said nothing. Then he covered his face with his hands.

I'm so sorry, I said, I'm so sorry for everything. I felt tremendous grief.

But I had no other words, there were no words that came to me that I could say.

I turned abruptly, my cheeks burned with shame as I remembered that later, and I left, left the room, I ran up the grass into the house.

I SPENT THE NEXT FEW MORNINGS in my studio looking at canvases, at paintings I had finished and put aside. I'd lift one, and put it up. I sat in my chair. I'd look at it, at the canvas, the morning light slanting along it. Then I'd lean my head against the chair back, and close my eyes. Then I'd look at another one.

Finally, after some days, and many hours, hours of solitude and beauty in the studio, I chose one. I chose it.

And I drove to André soon after, with the painting. It was a small one, from the group inspired by the river in Villiers, from the group Howard's painting came from. It was an abstract, oil.

The painting differed from Howard's, but it's hard to say how it differed. A slight variation in shading, in shade, in hue. A line that strayed in a different way. I'm not good with words.

How a painting by an artist can resemble another of hers, but differ from it, like siblings in a family. I've said before: I used to worry about repeating myself in my work, but I learned, I know now, that that's how it is, how it must be. Sameness, and difference: an endless pendulum between these two.

André admired the painting I had chosen for Joseph. We spent an afternoon choosing a frame, André brought out frame after frame, lighter ones and darker ones, heavier ones, then finer ones. He carried them back and forth, from his shelves behind him, then from his room at the back, while I sat up on a high stool (he had one like Eric's). André had such precise, careful hands. He'd hold; he'd measure. We shared words. I've said before: I trusted André.

It's André who chose the frame. He found a frame.

And a week later I picked it up.

I KEPT IT WITH ME in my bedroom, propped on the wall beneath its cloth cover, next to my bed. I kept it there for several days. I couldn't look at it, I didn't lift the cloth cover to look at it, but I didn't want to move it, or take it from there.

I slept better those few nights, I remember that. I felt I was sleeping next to a solved problem, I felt I had resolved something. But what had I resolved? Impossible to say, I cannot say.

And then, one cold afternoon, I took the painting covered with its cloth and carried it down the grass under my arm, to the garden room. I knocked on the door.

Joseph answered, at once. My breath came frosted, in a cloud, as I said: I have your painting. And I stepped in.

I'd had Josias carry down his toolbox and leave it at the garden room's door, the day before. André had attached the picture wire. Joseph and I would hang the painting, that was my plan.

Jacqueline, he said. I'm . . . and he turned away. He seemed lost for words. I lifted the cloth from the painting. I walked to his chair and pulled it out, and set the painting on it, propped against the chair's back. I stepped back, and gestured Joseph to join me. Here it is, I said.

We both stood looking at the painting. Joseph was silent for a long time.

I felt, in that moment, I must turn and embrace him, his wool sweater would scratch against my face.

It's the Vaal, the Vaal River, you know, I said.

I know, Joseph said. I know. He bowed his head and covered his face with his hands, in that movement I remembered from a few days before.

And instead of saying something, but saying what, what —
I fled, I fled the room. I ran up the grass, into the house, and
into my bedroom. And I wept.

I WOULDN'T HANG the painting. I couldn't. I had an idea it
was something I was incapable, incapable of doing.

I told Josias later to pick up his toolbox from its place
outside the door, and return it to the garage. I watched Josias
carry it up, it was an old battered thing, navy blue.

AND THEN WINTER started to turn. The grass was no longer white with frost in the mornings. Emily stopped making her soups.

I told Emily to wash the windows of the garden room, it doesn't look like you washed them long ago when I told you to, I said. I did ma'am, I did, they get dirty again, that's what happens, that's what happens to windows, she said. It sounded like a conversation my mother would have had with Emily, or with Maggie, I recognized it at once, as I spoke. I disliked myself then. I turned away.

My mother and father had not visited again, they didn't visit in winter and I made excuses when my mother asked if we'd come to Villiers. I pictured the dry yellow grass of my mother's garden, the cacti, the lizards in the cold sun. Perhaps Maggie had been drinking again. I didn't ask.

I've made another cover, a patchwork one, my mother told me on the phone. It'll go in Stephen's room, same colours as his room, she said. I thought at once that Stephen wouldn't like it, Stephen would be twelve soon, he was interested in his own things. He had his swimming trophies lined up on his desk, his chessboard, he was good at chess. He wouldn't want that patchwork on his bed.

Next time you come you'll see how tall he's grown, Mom, I said. That's all I said.

HOWARD HAD BEEN to the police station again, to enquire about Tiny. Her room was a space, a blank space now, in that backyard. I'd been in it, I'd seen it. Bare, the room. Quite bare. Nothing there. No trace of Tiny. Perhaps she'd never been there.

Howard told me about his latest conversation at the police station. The blank face of the young officer, and his boss this time, a thick-set man, standing behind him. No, *meneer,* the boss said, my people checked again, we got no record. No record of that person. There's lots of missing Blacks, *meneer,* we can't keep track of them and what you worried about, *meneer.* They look after themselves, I told you before. We got big work to do here, *meneer,* big problems here.

Howard returned home in a fury again, even more furious. I've said it before: Howard didn't often get angry.

I remember our conversation that night, I lying with my book, the lamp of my night-table, and Howard getting ready for bed.

It's intolerable, he said.

How's Joseph and the garden room? he said. He hadn't asked for a long time, he was busy and preoccupied with work, as I've said.

It's fine, I said. What does Jack Benator say, are they going to move him? This situation is what's intolerable, I said. I turned away.

AND ONE EVENING Emily returned from her day off in Alexandra and told me she'd heard news about Tiny. Tiny went to see her children, her mother, once, just once. She told them she was living with her boyfriend, somewhere else, she wouldn't say where. She had a job as a nanny again, that's what she said. She was alive, she was alive, Emily said. Beyond that: nothing, nothing else she knew.

Josias was standing there as Emily told me about Tiny. He clicked his tongue in that way he had. He shook his head. We said nothing, but I thought of Tiny's room, her empty, bare room. I thought of her figure, a young woman's figure, shapely beneath her blue uniform, her apron. I thought of her children, playing in the rutted roads of Alexandra township. Bare feet, in the dust.

AS IT BECAME WARMER, Josias started cleaning up the pool, which was green with algae, it had been under the grey tarpaulin for the winter. There was now the familiar sight of him and the pool net, sweeping, sweeping across the water. And the chlorine, the chlorine levels, to worry about. Howard drove Josias to the hardware shop and they came back with the chlorine, and a new chlorine measure. I imagined the two of them in the car, a conversation only about the chlorine, how much it was last time, how much it must be this time; what colour the measure must be this time, what colour it had been last time. Back and forth. Then silence. Howard driving. Josias in the front seat, looking out of the passenger window, the front windscreen. Josias was never in a car, when would he be in a car?

And in the hardware shop, the two of them going up and down the aisles, following each other, like friends. Or partners. And again: Howard talking about the chlorine last time, and what must be got this time. No *baas*, Josias would argue, this is the one; not that one. Then, a consultation with the shop assistant, who addressed himself only to Howard, not to Josias. And finally: the right chlorine found, the right measure, the right box. Josias carrying it ahead to the cash.

And home, a better mood for both of them this time on the way home. A job done. The pool would be ready for summer.

But one day soon after, the pool filter broke, and again the two of them had to set off one evening, back to the hardware store. I heard Josias speaking in his language afterwards in the kitchen with Emily: a string of words I didn't understand, and then 'filter'; more unintelligible words in his language, and 'filter.' 'Filter' again. A laugh then from Josias. Was he mocking Howard? I think so.

The filter, in any case, was fixed. The pool became clear: it glinted, a sapphire on some days, in the sun. I bought the children new swimsuits, they had grown so much.

I WENT TO my studio every morning, but I didn't work on my painting. It stood on its easel in the corner, but I had turned it around to face the wall, there was no point looking at it, I went nowhere, made no progress, doing that. I started working on some sketches though, which were minor things, drawings in pencil. I drew trees, mostly trees, and from memory, I never stepped out, say, into my garden, to draw with my sketch pad there. I'd also brought a book I had into the studio, a coffee-table book with photos of trees — encyclopaedic. Most often I drew (and drew, and re-drew) the thorn trees I knew from the Karoo, lone trees, sentinels in the dryness. I felt I was a thorn tree, then.

Josias did some planting. I didn't really know about gardening, what to plant, where, but I went to the nursery each spring, and bought trays of seedlings, small plantings, advised by the nursery owner. She knew me, and my garden. Mrs. Kline, here are your usuals, did your geraniums survive the winter? I wasn't sure, I hadn't noticed, but I'd listen to her, I took her suggestions. Nasturtiums? she said. And I'd come home with the trays in the trunk of my car, orange nasturtiums that I remember, soft, nodding blooms in the sun. Josias carrying them out and exclaiming and commenting on each one. His English had improved. He knew what the plants I brought were, he knew where they were going, and didn't need much direction from me. Soon enough I'd see him from the window deep in a flower bed with his spade, and then the hose which he hauled from the side of the house, and, later, he'd put the sprinkler on. The sheets of water curved, back and forth, back and forth, a rhythmic motion I watched.

I WENT TO SEE JOSEPH. I'd not been to see him since I had given him the painting, I worried about what he'd done with it. We hadn't hung it, and I imagined it in the place I'd last seen it, propped against the chair back (but he'd have to sit, and what about when one of his comrades came, and sat in the chair?)

I knocked, he came to the door. Jacqueline. I'm so glad to see you, he said, and he stepped aside to let me in. His table was crowded with charts, his papers. Overflowing papers and piles on the floor. His books. His bed rumpled, I hadn't seen that before. His dirty dishes in a pile on the floor. And my eyes scanned the room . . . the painting?

And then I saw it, it was propped on a small ledge on the wall. It was the right height, almost the height I would have hung it with the hammer and nail as I'd originally planned, and it was visible from the chair at the table.

And then I was overwhelmed. That's not a bad place for it at all, I said. My comrades love it, he said, and he laughed. Oh, that's excellent, I said. I looked at the painting. On that plain, peeling wall, on that small ledge, it looked quite strange.

Is everything else alright, I said. I felt so afraid to speak, I must not speak. Yes, it's fine, he said. I'm still here, right?

It was warm now, he no longer wore the navy sweater, he was in his white shirt again, open at the neck. He was perhaps thinner than before. How I wanted to lay my head on his white shirt, on his shoulder, it would be freshly laundered, an ironed smell — who was washing his clothes? I loved that white shirt.

I must go, I said, and I turned to the door.

Jacqueline, he said. Lie with me one day, he said. Lie with me here. I looked back at him in terror, it must have been terror. I fled, I fled again, that room.

And then I felt like a child. Like a small, frightened child.

THAT NIGHT I told Howard that Joseph really must go. It's a strain on us all, Howard, I said. The children. Benator really should have made a plan as he promised. And what if he's found? What will happen to us? Have you read the newspapers, Howard?

I know what's happening, Howard said, I know. He hasn't been found. He won't be found. It's been a safe place.

And I turned from Howard, again, in our bed.

AND MY DREAMS became inhabited with a white cotton shirt: a man's shirt. An ordinary man's shirt. A collar, unbuttoned, and white cuffs. A shirt, smelling of the iron, and the sun. Its purity filled my dreams.

HELENA ASKED ME on her last visit if it's too difficult for me now doing my laundry in the basement of our building — more worrying for her! And then I got angry with her. You're treating me like a child, Helena, I said. You're being ridiculous. I didn't tell her I've had my cleaning woman do my laundry for a while now.

Why that small deception? I don't know why. Perhaps I'm ashamed to be growing old.

IT WAS SOON the Christmas holidays, December of 1972. Joseph had been with us eleven months.

Josias asked for the month off to travel to his family in the Transkei. A month, I remember saying. What will happen with the pool, Josias? Josias opened his arms in a gesture of helplessness. My mother's sick, ma'am, he said. My mother's sick. Alright, alright, Josias. I figured out a time for him to go. December 1st? And you come back January 2nd, yes?

I had an idea he wouldn't come back, that he would vanish, as Tiny had. Perhaps he didn't like his job here? Perhaps he'd had enough of his small, concrete room, his narrow bed, the dogs, their fly-strewn bowls, Emily, the laundry line. Me. The pool and its filter; the long, slow afternoons with the pool net. His supper at night with Emily, under the green light at the back of the kitchen. And money sent home every month, to the Transkei. But then it occurred to me: how does he send it home? Is that where he goes on Thursdays, his day off, to the post office on Corlett Drive, with an envelope of money? Money from Howard. Not much money.

How had I not wondered this before?

I had seen the post office as I drove along Corlett Drive, its entrance for Blacks with its sign: 'NIE-BLANKES,' and a long line, a line of ragged nannies, of gardeners, standing in the sun, or under the awning. *Nie-blankes:* 'non-white.' A definition by negative: saying what something is by saying what it is not. How clear, how clear it is to me now. Here.

KERRY JAMES MARSHALL, whose exhibition Helena saw in New York: a study of identity defined by a negative. A study of identity defined by someone else. But Marshall's work is a rebuke, the strongest possible rebuke, of Black identity as defined by someone else. His work claims Black identity back for himself. Such a triumph; such a radical triumph.

I READ, I read a lot here. I don't paint any more, I gave up my studio a few years ago.

I had that studio for a long time. It was a high-ceilinged space, on the fourth floor. It had an old elevator with brass doors, the kind I know so well. I didn't use it. I'd walk up the stairs, old stairs, stained tile floors, a yellowed wall. But I was young, then.

I read a lot of non-fiction now, not only the fiction that was my lifelong habit. Ta-Nehisi Coates. It's an obligation, an obligation I feel to read. An atonement.

J OSIAS WENT TO SEE his mother in the Transkei. He left on December 1st, a boiling hot day, he came into the kitchen and had Emily call me, he wanted to tell me he was leaving, leaving now. I hope you're coming back, Josias, I said. I was only half joking. Yes ma'am, I'm coming back. Howard had given him his pay in advance, he was going to take the train from central Johannesburg. First he had to take the bus to get to the city. Along Corlett Drive, I saw that bus stop every day: crowded, a long line of people, waiting.

I followed Josias out into the yard, he was carrying two plastic bags. He was wearing the long pants I saw him in on his days off. The bags were the white ones from our grocer, I saw the logo on the side: Kyle & Anderson, Grocers. Is that all your luggage, Josias, I said. And then Josias and Emily had a quick exchange, in their language, small laughter between them. I think of that now, the three of us standing in the sun next to the laundry lines. My choice of word: luggage.

How much luggage would Josias have had? I feel embarrassed as I think of it.

Goodbye Josias, hope it's alright, hope your mother will be alright, I said. See you next year, I said, and I smiled. January 2nd, right? He bowed his head, sometimes he did that. He had some words with Emily then, as I turned away and went back into the house.

JOSIAS WAS GONE for a month, he did indeed return on January 2nd. Emily called me when he arrived, I went to the kitchen, the back, to find him drinking tea and eating bread, laughing with Emily, talking, talking. I felt such relief to see his familiar face, his lean figure, wearing the long pants. Even the children went in later, I could hear them bantering with him: nice holiday, Josias, did you enjoy your holiday?

I asked him how his mother was and he said, she's okay, she's an old lady, ma'am, an old lady. He nodded, as though thinking about her, about the old woman he had left. Because when would Josias get back there? I imagined an old woman, a country woman, I had seen women like that on the sides of roads near Villiers. She'd be standing, standing for a long time, watching Josias's thin figure start its long, slow walk down the dirt path, to the road, the walk along the long, winding road to Umtata in the distance, from where, hours later, he'd take the train, one long day on the train, to Johannesburg.

But I didn't really imagine that, where Josias had gone. The Transkei, the train, Umtata, his mother, the wide country-side he had traversed over many hours: they hardly existed in my mind, at all. I had a vague impression, more a feeling, of the wideness of our country, which I carried within me always; a vague instinct, or knowledge, about the 'home-lands,' where the Black people lived and came from. That's all. And I say 'our country.' It wasn't our country, all of ours: mine, Josias's, Emily's. It was a place that was taken, a people dispossessed. I knew that. I knew it because of my education; I knew it because I was married to Howard, who knew it. And there was Joseph: Joseph in our home, working night and day to overthrow the state itself, by all and any means necessary. I knew it.

I say I knew it because of my education. I mean my university education. At elementary and high school they didn't teach us that. They taught us nothing about colonialism; about dispossession; about what was really happening there, at all. In fact, they purposely hid it. They lied.

WHILE JOSIAS WAS AWAY Emily fed the dogs, and the neighbour's gardener cleaned our pool. I made the arrangement with our neighbour, a nice enough woman, she didn't mind. We paid the gardener for this directly, Howard gave him money every week. The pool wasn't as clean as usual, leaves accumulated and the children complained. Ah Mom, I come out of the pool covered in leaves, Stephen said. He was swimming lengths then, practising for his galas, for his swim team. Some afternoons Helena refused to go into the pool, pulling a face at the leaves floating over the surface. She'd lie instead on her towel and talk to her brother, interrupting his lengths, and bothering him. Sometimes she'd just stay inside the house in her room, with a book.

Howard looked after the chlorine, I'd see him fiddling with the measure, then bending over the filter, frowning, in the evenings. I suppose you could say that we missed Josias.

WE DIDN'T GO AWAY to the sea as we usually did, that year at Christmas. Howard was worried about work, he'd become so busy he had to go to his study after dinner and work, for a few more hours. We seldom sat at night any more, having coffee or tea on the patio. He had new clients, large steel companies, and another company affiliated with Anglo American, I think he became indispensable to some corporations, some executives, who relied on him exclusively. And there was now a government client, a major branch of a transportation portfolio (as he explained it to me). I didn't really understand it all, or care, until later, later, when it became relevant. Relevant to everything.

But I think Howard also feared leaving the house for two weeks, with Joseph, Joseph alone at the house. Leaving Joseph undefended. What if something happened, a neighbour came by, or an intruder, and police were called, and . . . then what? I'd had vague thoughts about that myself. But Howard would never have said this to me, he knew how enraged I'd become. That we should miss our annual holiday because of the man Jack Benator had left here, for far too long? Howard felt some guilt I think, about the impact it was having on us all.

The children were disappointed about not going to the sea, the highlight of their year. I loved the sea, that place with its white beaches, its surf, its roar. I imagined my feet in the sand as we climbed the dune, rough scrub around us, a ragged wind. The smell, the sting of salt on my cheeks. And so wide, that beach, that sea. I always looked with wonder at the horizon, thinking, if I could see and see and see, I would

144

see across the entire width of the Indian Ocean. The Indian Ocean stretched from our shore.

In the drawer of my dressing table I had the blue stone I'd found in a shop, I'd take it out in my room and hold it up to the light. In Johannesburg, the sea existed as a shimmering blue in my mind, not the blue of the sea, but the blue of a kind of peace. We didn't feel at peace, that year.

So we decided to go to Villiers for a few days, just a few days, to visit my parents, and for the children to have some time in a different place, and swim in the river. Villiers wasn't far. My father promised Stephen fishing, they'd go in a rowboat, fishing.

But before that Howard's firm had a party for the holidays. It was at the Benators' house.

IT WAS A PARTY like all the others, the others we went to, Howard and I, that I haven't mentioned much. I didn't care for them, I've said so.

A pool under the summer stars, drinks and clinking glass, some music wafting from the lit windows of the house. I sat on a deck-chair with my drink, Howard was talking to some people, clients I suppose, that I didn't know. There was a woman laughing in a loud and crude way, I put my head back then against the chair cushion, and closed my eyes.

I thought of Villiers, where we'd go soon. I thought of the peach trees, and the swing where Helena would swing, as I'd done as a child. I thought of the rough blanket that I'd haul out and lie on, as I looked up to the blue, cloudless sky. I'd bring a book. Perhaps I'd also bring my sketch pad, although I never carried it with me. No, I wouldn't bring my sketch pad. I've said how I used to hide it when I was a child, and I had the same instinct now. There'd be comments. Those trees look so real, Jacqueline! My trees were just exercises, diversions for me, from my painting that had died, on its easel.

And Howard. Howard would get some rest in Villiers. He'd go with my father to his shop, he enjoyed doing that. They'd talk business: the price of lumber, the price of steel, my father bought and sold lumber. The lumber yard was behind my father's shop, a wide space of unpaved ground, under the hot sun. I'd always avoided that yard. It wasn't a place for a child, or a girl. Mountains of lumber, dust, Black men shouting, or lounging under the eaves, on their rest.

Then I thought of Howard and my father, and their other favourite subject: the rugby. This player or that one, this rugby match or that one. The Springboks, in their green and gold jerseys. Such proprietary pride my father felt, towards the Springboks. *Bokke.* He'd listen to a match broadcast from Ellis Park in Johannesburg on the small black radio he carried around with him. I'd hear the familiar voice of the broadcaster, excitement mounting through the crackling across the air-waves, and through the small radio, which my father would then put to his ear. Howard would listen with my father, they'd banter about it, this could occupy hours. I sometimes thought Howard was merely humouring, even indulging my father, and in a way I think he was. That was Howard's way, too.

The shop next to the lumber yard was a cavernous building, filled with shelves, floor to ceiling, of . . . everything. Blankets, soap, buckets, dresses, hats, dishes. Black people from sur-rounding farms came into the shop and bought things, they were the bulk of my father's customers. But Afrikaans women from the town were customers too. White women in their prim, print dresses, their heels, their stockings. Sometimes they expressed disdain, I see disdain now in their faces, as I remember them. Perhaps that's not fair, but I think it's true.

Their dresses, their stockings, their pale faces: they were not unlike my mother. But my mother was not an Afrikaner.

I WAS INTERRUPTED in my thoughts, my thinking about Villiers, by a voice. Mrs. Kline, Mrs. Kline, I've been looking for you. Howard said you'd be here, at the pool! And I opened my eyes to see Candace walking towards me, Candace in higher heels than I'd seen her wear at the office, Candace teetering, in a pale peach-coloured dress, towards me.

Oh Candace, I said, and I stood up at once, and smoothed my skirt, I wore a skirt and blouse, how is it that I remember, so clearly? It was a silky blue skirt, it reached to my knees. The blouse was another shade of blue, also silk, a buttoned shirt, tucked in. Perhaps I wore that because it was Howard's office party. It wasn't a cocktail outfit, most of the women were in cocktail outfits. But I liked that skirt and shirt, I'd had it for years.

Mrs. Kline, she said. I've been telling everyone about the beautiful art you put in our office. Such a beautiful picture, Mrs. Kline, she said. I felt the rush of warmth towards Candace again, it was such a small canvas, she'd paid it such close attention. Thank you, Candace. And then I looked at her and said, did you ever study art? Oh, no, she said. But I think I'd like to. I used to like drawing when I was a child. Well, me too, you know, I said. I smiled. I suddenly felt protective of Candace. I thought of her sitting at her desk, in that sober reception room, the suited men that must walk through those doors. The long days, of that, just that. Ushering suited men into Howard's office, Jack Benator's office, Jones's office. And then: making tea. Carrying in trays of tea. Howard, or Benator, or some other man would say then, thank you, Candace. And out she'd go again through the door, shutting it behind her. I thought of Emily.

You know, Candace, I think you should take some art lessons, just for fun you know, take some lessons. She looked at me in astonishment, as though this had never occurred to her before. Yes Mrs. Kline, but I have to save money, I'm still living with my parents, I must save money so one day I can get a flat, move out. Get married, she said. And she laughed. Of course, I said. I thought then of the men in suits, or other men, looking at Candace, up and down, up and down. Candace's young, beautiful body. Perhaps I can think of someone who teaches art, I said.

And then, Jack Benator was walking towards us. In casual clothes, an open-necked shirt, he our host, that evening. I was telling Mrs. Kline how much we love her painting, Mr. Benator, she said. Ah, he said. Wonderful. She's fantastic. She's going to be famous one day, I've got my money on her, he said, and we all laughed. How much money, said Candace, and we laughed again.

Will you have another drink, Jacqueline, Jack said, Candace? My glass, it is true, was empty. So I turned with Jack Benator towards the table with drinks on the other side of the pool, and Candace said, no thanks, I'm going to use the ladies', and Jack and I were then, suddenly, alone.

Joseph Weiss, he said. A pause. Your house has been remarkably safe for him. We're very grateful, many people are grateful to you and Howard, Jacqueline. You know that? He was speaking in a low voice, of course, and no one was near us, just the edge of the listening pool, and the trees bowing, alongside.

Jack, I said. And I felt the familiar fluttering, the alarm, at the reminder of this strange secret — our garden — the thought of it coming into my mind and filling it, again. It's been very difficult, I said. The children. What if he's found? I said. I thought he was going to be moved. Isn't it better to move him around? And then, hearing my own soft voice saying these things, at this ordinary party at a pool, I froze. I would say nothing more. And Howard? Howard would be annoyed with my talking like this to Jack Benator.

I have an idea Jack hardly heard me, or if he did, he brushed aside my words, in his mind. We're very grateful, Jacqueline, they're doing their best to find another place for him, they're doing their best.

This may well have been true. I felt superficial and selfish, then.

It's all fine, Jack, I said. This is a lovely party, Jack, your girls are lovely, I said then. His two small daughters had made an appearance earlier at the party, they'd come in, in their nightdresses, to be introduced and say goodnight. Two girls with long, fair hair, brushed carefully, for bed. They were a little younger than Helena.

After the party I sat in the car as Howard drove us home, and said nothing about Jack Benator. I've said before: I don't like parties.

IT WAS TIME to go to Villiers. Emily had instructions to take Joseph his meals, as before. Just be careful, I said to Emily. I'm not sure what I meant, I meant, don't tell anybody, don't let anyone down into the garden, what else could I have meant? We'd cancelled the neighbours' gardener cleaning our pool while we were away. Emily nodded. Emily understood.

What would we have done without Emily?

And I went to say goodbye to Joseph. Why did I do that? It was only a few days we'd be away, I had sometimes not seen Joseph for two, or three weeks, at a stretch. But I had to tell Joseph we were going away, I didn't want to leave that to Emily, to tell, to explain all that, to him.

His words, the words he'd said to me on my last visit, I still carried with me, in a secret space — another secret space — in my mind. How many secret spaces I had now, that I'd never had, before. Lie with me, Jacqueline, he had said. And for the first time it occurred to me: did he mean, tell a lie? To lie with him would be a lie. Then again, it came to me: to lie with him would be a deep truth.

No, he didn't mean tell a lie. He meant what I'd first understood, I knew it, of course I knew it.

I knocked on his door, and how I remember the exact sound of that soft knocking on the old, wooden door, under the shade of the trees, the exact, filtered light, a faint rustle of birds, a start of a bird, perhaps. A tableau. I, standing at the worn step, in that glade. If I still painted, I'd paint it. But I never painted figures, you know that. No, I would never have painted that.

And Joseph's immediate opening of the door, he standing there, his dark head, his bearded face, his glasses.

But that day Joseph wore a different shirt, it was a pale blue one, a collared, buttoned shirt, like the white one. The same shirt, just a different colour.

Joseph, I said, I'm not coming in. We're going away, to Villiers, for five days. Me. Howard. The children. Emily will carry on with everything, as before.

And then he said: Villiers? On the Vaal?

Yes, I said, my parents live there.

Your painting, he said.

Yes, yes, my painting, that is true, I said. We both smiled.

Is everything else alright, Joseph, I said. Yes, yes, all is fine, he said. He gestured towards his table, covered, as always, with his papers, and the pile of books, on the floor. Joseph, while we're away you should go out into the sunshine a bit you know, just step out, I said. Ah, he said. He shook his head. It's alright, Jacqueline, don't worry.

Goodbye then, I said, and I reached to shake his hand.

Shake his hand? I had not shaken his hand since the evening I'd met him, almost a year before. Such a formal gesture. But he reached out, and we shook hands. His hand was firm and strong, and dry, I remember it. A man's hand, only a man's hand felt that way.

And then I turned, and walked, quickly, up the grass. I feel he must have been standing there, watching me, my departing self: my pale legs, my sandals, my skirt.

WE WENT TO VILLIERS. We drove that familiar road, out of the city, past the mine dumps. A city ringed with mine dumps, strange pale hills, dusky: the dun residue of gold. Gold. We felt it then, but I know it now: they, the mine dumps, were the source, the reason, for everything. The state was built upon it: the state itself.

I thought of Joseph then. I thought of the charts, the maps, the work at night. I thought of the article I'd read just that week, about an explosion in a small mine, on the West Rand. Machinery damaged, no person injured; the mine disabled for four days.

I said nothing to Howard driving in the car, nothing about these thoughts. Perhaps he was thinking about similar things, but I don't know. Maybe he was just concentrating on the road; perhaps he was worrying about a work problem. Perhaps that is true.

But the children were happy, first bantering, then arguing in the back seat. Chester and Teddy know we're going away, Stephen said, did you see how they were jumping and barking when we left? Helena laughed. They'll miss us, she said. No, they won't miss *you,* Stephen said. Only me. And then Helena was upset and I had to intervene: a familiar scene, in our family.

There wasn't much traffic. We drove.

And then: flat space. The veld, stretching yellow-brown into the distance, some shanties, and a lone figure walking along the side of the road. I've said before: I only saw beauty in that landscape later, other artists had seen beauty in it forever, but I, not I. A mangy dog, an abandoned dog. A long, straight road, to the Free State.

Free State. I didn't think of the irony, then.

And the towns we passed: Vereeniging; Vanderbijlpark, Sasolburg. The sign for Kroonstad, then we knew we were close. And then: the bridge over the Vaal. My heart lifted. The river. How I loved that river. Its strange pale brownness; its power. I always imagined its long journey, so many miles more that we couldn't see, through and across veld, that vast swath, passing small *kopjes,* and a solitary thorn tree, one of the thorn trees that I tried to draw. The beauty that I later saw.

WE REACHED VILLIERS, and I felt as though I'd come home. Of course, I had.

We arrived at the house, Maggie came out as she heard the car doors opening, slamming, and the children's excited voices. Maggie, who looked more frail, more vague, than ever. Even diminished somehow, in size, and stature, her thin legs, the slippers she wore, inside and out. Or perhaps that's because I'd known Maggie since she was a young woman, first come to work for my mother. A young woman whose English was non-existent at the beginning. My mother had been her first employer. My mother thought Maggie came from the country, some place, some place my mother didn't know. Or perhaps, she said, she came from the Location, the sprawling shanty town on the road leading to Villiers. My mother didn't really know. And the Location: a mysterious place to me, it always glinted in its flat, dull way in the sun, as we drove past.

Maggie had arrived one day at my mother's garden gate. Job, she said. My mother was standing on her porch, in the shade of her porch. 'Job' was the only English word Maggie knew. And my mother hired her.

How do I know this, how do I know how Maggie arrived? Because my mother told me, years later. When I was an adult, and had asked her. Where did Maggie come from? Who was Maggie?

My mother brought a blue uniform and white apron, a white head scarf, a *doek,* home, she brought it home from my father's shop, he did brisk business selling maids' uniforms to the white women employers, in town. The Afrikaans women. My mother was not an Afrikaner: I've said that before.

My mother showed Maggie the small room in the back-yard, an iron bed was brought by a man from my father's shop, some milk crates pushed together for a table.

That was Maggie's room.

And something very important: where did Maggie get her name, I asked my mother that too, when I was an adult — a mother — myself.

I — I gave her her name, my mother said. She didn't have one, I mean I don't know what her name was, she couldn't tell me, she didn't speak English, and she said nothing at all for many weeks, just followed me around, as I showed her everything.

I wondered about that, about Maggie's name. Give someone a name? It seemed so much more important than we — my mother — understood it to be.

Maggie's English hardly improved. Perhaps Maggie didn't like to speak, I feel that speaking cost her too much, too much energy, too much . . . something, I don't know what. I feel she was an inward person, but what is an inward person? And what was within her? I don't know.

Maggie would go out on her day off, my mother thought she went to the Location, and she'd come back again in the evening. A long walk it would have been, to the Location, along a hot, straight road. How else would Maggie have gone there? I think about that, now.

And Maggie developed a problem with drink, as I've said. Over the years. It wasn't so evident in the beginning. She drank meths, meths was cheap, it cost nothing, a bottle of methylated spirits, you could get it in any shop. It had a sharp, a terrible smell, I remember it. We: I, my mother, my father, knew instantly when Maggie was drinking. Those fumes, that smell, was the smell of our home, too.

Maggie was a person carrying absences. The vagueness when she was drunk, her inability — or unwillingness — to speak in our language, held a truth: the truth of erasure within her. But this insight is one I've only had over the years, and here. I told you: I read Ta-Nehisi Coates, and others. I'm an admirer of Kerry James Marshall, whose exhibition Helena saw last month.

But that year, in December of 1972, we arrived in Villiers, our family in our car, happily, to visit my parents. There was Maggie's faint smile, as she greeted us with a nod of her head, and moved to the trunk to help us carry out our bags.

But I think she had less strength in her arms than the children did, so it was they and Howard who were carrying the bags and suitcases, and she just fluttered along beside them, like a bird.

HOWARD AND I SLEPT in the room I'd had as a girl. Now it had two narrow beds pushed together, so two people could sleep there. There was a net curtain at the window, the window which overlooked the peach trees, and the circular washing line, hanging with white sheets, with sheets: how many sheets did Maggie wash, in her lifetime? There was no washing machine in that house, just the stone sink, large, that I'd see filled with soapy water, Maggie bending over it with the washboard, back and forth, back and forth, as she washed the sheets, the clothes. And then, the hanging on the line. Maggie had more strength in her arms than I thought.

I could imbue those motions over the washboard, the clothesline, with beauty, make a painting of them. But I never, ever did. You know that, there is no such painting in my work, no such tableau. Then again, I've never done figurative work, my paintings are abstract. So I leave it with the critics, the journalists, to say what they see. They have said it, too.

You can make beauty out of any ugliness, any great sin, and the question is why, why would you do it? Why must you do it? And what is left, when you have made it — a beautiful thing — out of ugliness?

What, what have I left?

HOWARD BROUGHT a box of special cigars for my father, sometimes he did that. There was a cigar shop on Rissik Street, a dark shop with a humidor and crimson walls, I'd been past it. Howard didn't smoke but he'd have a cigar with my father, then they'd go out onto the porch together and sit, beside my mother's miniature cacti on their stands, and smoke, and talk, looking out towards the iron gate, and the empty grey street, beyond. A street in a small country town. My mother would complain about the smell, my father's pipe was one thing, she said, but cigars . . .

I had brought my mother the copy of Nadine Gordimer's story collection, a hardcover, ochre-coloured. My mother would enjoy it. And a puzzle, then. How is it that my mother enjoyed Nadine Gordimer, who wrote about apartheid, when she was ignorant and oblivious of the structure of the country around her, the meaning of it?

Something I understood only years later: my mother recognized the real world in Nadine Gordimer's stories, she appreciated the realism, the vivid realism of the stories. The books described my mother's world. But the imperative contained within the works: the search for and advocating of a new state; the profound moral critique; the desire and search for justice; these, these all, escaped my mother. I may be wrong, but I don't think so. My mother was not educated beyond high school.

You could understand it less benevolently. Perhaps my mother was simply lazy, and enjoyed her comfortable life, and wouldn't have wanted to give it up. Worse, maybe she derived a perverse satisfaction from the uneven, unequal relationship she had with Maggie, and couldn't imagine losing it. I don't know which of these understandings or interpretations is true, or more true, and so I have to conclude that they may all be true.

BUT WE ALL RELAXED in Villiers, those closing days of 1972.
Joseph in the garden room receded from my mind. But
then I'd remember him, with a start, and it was like remem-
bering a distant nightmare. Once, in a dream, there was his
white shirt, its ironed smell.

The children went swimming with Howard and my father
in the river. They'd leave with whoops of joy, in their swimsuits and flip flops, their towels over their shoulders. My father
didn't swim, but Howard did. It gave me pleasure to imagine
them, on the banks of the river, lying on that rock, amidst
other children, the Afrikaans children, and under the glinting
sun, splashing in the water, the willows overhanging alongside.

There were boats too, rowing boats, a slow row around
the quieter shallows of the river, I can still hear the clunk of
the heavy wooden oars against the side.

My mother and I were left at the house. I told her I wanted to
read my book, and I took the blanket, spread it on my mother's
grass, near the rocks, a black lizard rustling as I lay down.

My mother pottered among her roses, wearing gardening
gloves and carrying her scissors, she carefully cut, cut, she
was pruning, or tidying, I suppose. Her heels, her low heels,
sinking into the dry grass as I watched.

And later she would be in the kitchen supervising Maggie,
who was getting dinner ready. A leg of lamb dinner, in the
dining room. Potatoes. The children loved those dinners.

They loved the breakfasts too, not cereal and orange juice
as Emily prepared them at home, but fried eggs, *boerewors,*
fried tomatoes. They ate a lot, we all sat at the kitchen table
for breakfast, noisy children, children on holiday, Howard

relaxed and talking, I reading the paper. But my parents didn't get the *Rand Daily Mail,* the paper we got at home. The newspaper my parents read was no good, it was almost certainly under the influence and control of state censors. It was also in Afrikaans. I'd forgotten they didn't read the same newspaper as we did, and I put the paper aside, I wouldn't read it.

Mom, you should get the *Rand Daily Mail,* I said. Dad's happy with this newspaper, no reason to change newspapers, she said. There was no point arguing.

I slept well in my room, my old room, it still had its large heavy dresser, the dressing table with mirrors, like the one I had at home. And a large old wardrobe, filled with dresses, the dresses I had worn when seventeen, eighteen, and nineteen years old. Why did my mother keep them? They were on their hangers, nestled up against each other, so many of them. Their colours: pinks, and yellows, and blues and greens, rustling crinolines. A white one, tulle. And some silk patterned ones. In bell shapes, and cinched waists, the fashions of 1959. I wore them during the years I was at university, in Johannesburg.

There were the visits to Mrs. Hanekom's shop: to Mrs. Hanekom, who made those dresses. She made most of my dresses, and had taught my mother to make other, simpler ones for me too.

Mrs. Hanekom's shop was small and crammed with hats, many hats, the hats women wore to church, in Villiers.

I'd never set foot in a church.

THERE WAS A SMALL SYNAGOGUE in a town near Villiers. We went on the holidays, although my father went more often, sometimes on Saturday mornings. The synagogue was in a low building, its small Star of David centred on the roof above the front door. Inside, there were stained glass windows, like jewels, deep blues and reds and gold, which glowed deeply when the sun shone through them. There were gilt-and-velvet canopies, and crimson velvet cloths, and Hebrew lettering, and men in their blue-and-white shawls, praying, in a low murmur of that old language.

The women sat upstairs, I'd sit next to my mother, wearing a dress she or Mrs. Hanekom had made, sometimes with a small, white jacket that I remember. My mother would glance down at me approvingly, as I sat holding the dark blue prayer book, its Hebrew, black script, pages and pages of it, inside. The other women and girls whispered, like birds, I felt we were observers only, as we looked down on the men below, the tops of their heads, their blue-and-white prayer shawls, their murmurings.

When you stepped out of the small, jewelled interior of that synagogue, you were standing on a wide grey street, under a pale blue sky, with nothing, and no one there. A Black man loitering on a corner, that's all.

A FEW WEEKS AGO I had occasion to be in a synagogue in New York, and as I sat holding a dark blue prayer book, closed, I deciphered the Hebrew lettering on the glowing windows at the front: Reuben, Simeon, Levi, Asher, Naphtali, Gad. Judah. The twelve tribes. Their brother, you know, is Joseph.

I read, the Hebrew letters were within me, I could read

them, still. My father had taught me to read Hebrew, and I remembered, suddenly, his face, his glasses, that glinted as he turned, turned the pages of the book, and had me repeat, repeat, the words, the letters, until I knew them.

THE HATS IN Mrs. Hanekom's shop came in every shape, and in every colour. There were pastels, some adorned with nets and others with glossy bows. The hats festooned that space like flowers. Mrs. Hanekom also had shelves of fabric, shelves and shelves, she had to stand on a ladder to reach them.

Mrs. Hanekom, always with her tape measure. And I, a slight, pale figure, standing at the mirror at the back of the shop.

A customer, an Afrikaans woman in dress and heels, coming in, the bell above the door clanging as it opened, inter-rupting us. And I'd have to stand at the mirror, waiting for Mrs. Hanekom to be done with the customer, *dankie mevrou, baie goed mevrou, okay, totsiens, totsiens mevrou.* And my mother then too, a few words in Afrikaans with the customer, whom she knew: *Lekker om jou te sien, groete aan die familie, Anneline.*

And then, back to me: the tape measure. Mrs. Hanekom's firm, feminine hands. *So mooi 'n meisie is jou,* she'd say. And my mother suggesting, commenting, speaking to Mrs. Hanekom, a red tulle this time, lovely! I said nothing.

I had worn one of the dresses, a pale blue one, to a dance with Howard, that was one of our first dates. Falling in love with Howard. I remembered it.

The dresses hung and rustled as I touched them then in the wardrobe, all those years later, their bell skirts jostling for room, like girls. I pushed the wardrobe door shut.

Aᴀ ᴛᴇʀ ᴛʜᴇ ᴇᴡ ᴅᴀYꜱ ɪN ᴠɪʟʟɪᴇRꜱ we drove home to Johannesburg. We got home late on a Sunday afternoon, the children tired and happy, they still had school holidays for a while, they would see some of their friends, swim in the pool, that week. Howard, especially, seemed revived. He'd lost his preoccupied look, and laughed and played more readily with the children. Emilyyyyyyy!! the children called, Chester!!!!! Teddy!!!! The dogs bounded to greet us, Emily came out of her room in the yard, she wasn't in her uniform, she wore a brown skirt, a blouse, the only one I'd ever seen her wear, when not in her uniform.

We were home.

And Joseph. Everything alright with Joseph, Howard asked. Yes, Emily said. I just carried on with the meals, with the food. All the same with Joseph, she said. I felt a small release, some part of me must have been worried, and I think Howard too. Who knows what might have happened in our absence? The men still coming at night to pick him up, Emily? I asked. Oh, yes, same-same, she said. Just the same. Wake me up every time, the dogs, but is fine, is fine.

Perhaps, I thought, I would visit my painting again. My painting, so long abandoned, some days I didn't think of it at all.

ᴀᴛᴇR ᴊᴏꜱɪᴀꜱ ᴄᴀMᴇ ʜᴏMᴇ on January 2nd, I felt we were complete, our family. Our household. I thought of us as ship-wrecked survivors, of a strange and violent storm. I had no idea what was still to come.

And the next week I went to see Eric. I'd not been for a while. He was stacking boxes on a ladder at the back of the store when I came in, and I felt a rush of gratitude for him, for his friendship. I'd missed him, I thought.

I've not been painting at all, I said, explaining, I thought, my long absence. Eric made us tea, his milky, mine black, and brought a plate of his biscuits. We settled on his high chairs, and the shop, as usual, was quiet. It was ours, our space. Then a woman came in, a customer, and Eric had to answer some questions from her, help her find something, while I sat alone on my chair and sipped my tea.

And then we caught up on each other's news. My news, all my news, except for my secret, our secret, the secret in the corner of our lives, at the end of my garden. I talked about the stasis with my painting. It's terrible, I told Eric. I told him about the sketches, the pencil sketches, my diversion: my trees. That's alright, he said, what else can you do? He had been through fallow periods as well, perhaps every artist has. And Eric was still making his way. He took out some sketches of his own, studies for paintings. His hand was firm; they were good. He had an interest in figures, he drew figures in motion, figures at rest; figures in various states of undress; of dress. But his grasp of anatomy was strong, his sense of rhythm too. I told him so. We spent a companionable hour that way. I felt strengthened by it as I said goodbye, and drove home, slowly, slowly along the streets.

That's how my afternoons used to be, I thought, before.

Before Joseph came.

MY MORNINGS, with the newspaper, were the same. My interest in the paper was still the small report I would seek, and occasionally find, like a nugget: an explosion on a small road near a power line; a problem, a mysterious problem, or attack, at a police station. Sabotage. Something like that. They weren't large explosions, they weren't major installations, they were at smaller power stations, or at smaller mines, in peripheral towns. But it was a beginning. I understood that now.

As I sat on my patio under the leaves which filtered the morning sun, and watched the pool in front of me, spread in promise and beauty, I could feel our days number. It was impossible to forget the man behind the trees, invisible, but there, working, working. I imagined I heard the scratch of his pen, as he wrote, wrote. I did not hear it.

I began to feel Jack Benator would never move Joseph, perhaps there'd never been a serious effort to move him, it was working too well.

Then I started to think I was to blame: to blame for making it work so well, so well that my family was now stuck with Joseph forever. If only I had made more of a fuss, been stronger with Howard. (I was never strong with Howard.) If only I'd insisted on him being moved, by saying it was dangerous for my children. (It was dangerous for my children.) It was surely my fault, as my children's mother. It was my fault.

I began to feel I should take things — something — into my own hands. Perhaps, I thought, I would finally be strong with Howard.

I would say: Howard, this is it. We never asked to harbour a fugitive, you did Jack a favour. I know we believe in his work, but it's enough, we've done enough. It is not safe for the children, or for us. You know it. I'm telling you now: have Joseph moved.

How I repeated that conversation, that rebellion of mine, in my mind. Like a tape on repeat, it went on and on, the same, the same words, circling in my mind, saying them emphatically to Howard. I imagined saying them in our room, as we were going to bed, I under my lamp, with my book. I imagined Howard's distracted face, as I said them.

But I never said the words aloud, or I never said them quite the way I imagined saying them, or with quite the emphasis, or with quite the . . . courage. Did I lack courage? Did I lack energy? Did I always lack those things?

My fault, my fault, again.

EMILY CAME ONE DAY with news of Tiny. It wasn't much news. Tiny had visited her children again. Tiny had a different job now, she said, and a different boyfriend. But Tiny was alive, alive. Those were Emily's words, Emily's word: alive. Emily shook her head as she told me. I had decided, long before, that I wasn't going to hire another maid to replace Tiny, not ever. My mother said to me several times, on the phone, have you got a new maid yet? You need one. The children. The laundry.

I'm not getting a new maid, I remember telling my mother. Perhaps I was reaching my limit, already then, my limit with everything.

I started visiting Eric at his store every week again. I'd asked him to suggest someone who gave art lessons, I was thinking of Candace. I didn't know where Candace lived and she worked full-time hours, but perhaps if I found her someone, she could make a plan for herself. Eric had some suggestions, some phone numbers, I would give them to Candace. Or, I would give them to Howard, he could pass them along to Candace.

And my painting: stasis. I took it out again from under its covering one day, and set the easel up where I could see it best, in the morning light. This time, however, I was startled to see that — how can I explain this — something in it had changed. Or moved. I tried to see what it was, why it now seemed to contain some beat of life, which it had lost, before.

It was like finding a bird on the ground, one long thought dead, but now with a heartbeat, a faintly quivering side, so faint a movement it was easy to miss it.

And then I realized it was all within me, every movement within myself, every small change, was reflected, or projected, onto my painting. A new projection was possible, I saw that now. There was hope for it.

Was it because of this, this renewal of energy within myself, a lifting of something, that I visited Joseph again? Why else, why did I visit Joseph again? Nothing was new or different in his situation, everything was just as before. I hadn't resolved with Howard, with Jack, about Joseph leaving, I hadn't been firm, as I'd wanted to be. Joseph was still there.

L AST WEEKEND Helena came again. Helena has taken the whole year off, she says they'll hold her job. I was alarmed when I heard this, but she says she's had enough, she wants a break, she wants to take time to decide what to do next. She's been teaching for twenty-five years, she reminds me. Nicholas is at university, and she says she feels free. Her husband Mark is a potter and owns his shop, a craft shop that sells his work and that of other local artists: pottery; paintings and small sculptures too. Tourists are his customers, Howard and I used to enjoy visiting, in the early days. Howard would drive us up there, we'd take a few days, we stayed at a local inn, the owner got to know us.

And I was a visiting artist myself then, Mark would introduce me, Helena would introduce me, they were very proud.

But: Helena taking all this time off work. I have a feeling it has something to do with me. She denied it vehemently when I suggested it, but I've said it before: she's worried about me. I don't walk as well as I used to, that is true, and this means I'm sometimes house-bound, stuck in my apartment. Helena has taken to calling me every day, every morning. This annoys me. There's no reason for her to worry about me, I've told her many times.

I'm not worried, Mom, she says, I'm just calling to say hi. There's no use pointing out that she never used to call me every day, it's a new thing, there's no point saying it. She'll find another answer, another reason to say why she's calling. So I've stopped protesting.

This time she arrived on Friday evening, and she went home on Tuesday morning. Again I was alarmed, or let's say uncomfortable, when she called to tell me her plan. But why for so long, Helena, I said. Doesn't Mark need you at home? I felt ridiculous as I said this, I knew it sounded ridiculous. She laughed. Well, who can blame her.

And then she said: d'you still have jars of the bone broth in your freezer? And the truth is, I realized with a start, I had forgotten the jars in the freezer. She had left other things in the freezer too: bags of chicken she had cooked; rice in meal-size portions, that kind of thing. I've said before: I've never eaten much, and I eat less now. And then I thought: yes, she's worried I don't eat. But I said then, in a sharp tone which I remember now, Helena, don't be silly, I'm not talking about food with you, I'm just not. She sighed.

She moved on to tell me, a little distantly, which train she was taking. And then she said goodbye, and I found myself standing alone in my hallway, the cell phone's small weight in my hand.

And I remembered then Helena as a teenager, and the conversations I'd have with her, the arguing about small things, her slamming doors and stamping off to her room. I didn't ask for your opinion, it's my outfit, she'd say, door slamming. It felt like that now, except that I was acting like a teenager, and she, the mother. I felt ashamed, and I suddenly wished Howard was here. Howard who could always calm me down; Howard who could defuse any argument in our house.

And there's something else Helena's worried about. She's worried that I don't carry my cell phone, or that I'll lose my cell phone, or that I don't charge my cell phone.

The truth is, I have forgotten to charge the cell phone

on occasion, the charger is plugged in next to my bed, but I forget, I forget to check it and charge it. Helena has got very angry about that.

And I should mention Stephen, Stephen harasses me about that too. Once when I forgot to charge my phone, Stephen had to come here, he had to get a cab from across the park, because Helena called him from Waterbury and said, where's Mom, I can't reach her. Stephen arrived at my door looking distracted and upset. Mom, no one can reach you, this is insane. Even Marie was called at work by Helena, he said. He marched into my bedroom, to where my charger was, pulled it out of its socket and brought it to me. You have to charge your phone, I can't do this in the middle of a work day, he said. And of course I felt guilty then, and ashamed.

But I was never good with details, even when I was young. It's not a detail, Mom, Helena said in exasperation, when I said that.

Then she pointed out that I was meticulous with my work — with my paintings. Meticulous, she said. And I couldn't deny it.

BUT HELENA ARRIVED on Friday evening. She'd told me her train was leaving Waterbury at 10:10 that morning, Mark would drive her to the station. And then she sent me an email with a link to the Amtrak site and the route of the train. Why did she do that? It's only by chance that I saw and opened that email. But then, as I sat in my chair facing the window, a bitter cold day, snow piled on the ground, even here in New York, I looked at my cell phone, at the link, and the route of the train.

I knew that route, Howard and I had travelled it many times

as I've said, in the car. I loved the names of the towns, I remembered how I'd always loved the names. And I followed them now,
on the map on my phone: Montpelier; Randolph; White River
Junction; Claremont; Bellows Falls; Brattleboro; Greenfield;
Northampton; Holyoke; Springfield; Hartford; Bridgeport;
Stamford; New Rochelle. They weren't the South African names
of the journeys of my childhood, and my young adulthood. They
were, they are, American names. Well, of course they are. Why
so compelling? I sat for a long time then, with my head leaning
against the back of the armchair, my eyes closed, and imagined
Helena's train journey, through all those towns. A bitter winter
journey, so much deep snow along the way. Fields of whiteness, hills, mounds of whiteness, a station master in Holyoke
stamping his boots in the cold, his breath a white cloud.

What a cold winter this has been.

And I imagined Helena's arrival at Penn Station, the train
pulling in to that cavernous place, and the passengers: New
York! Helena pulling her wheeled bag as she bumped down
and exited the train, her coat, her black coat that I knew, her
hat, black too, a bright blue scarf perhaps. A small figure.
Helena is not tall.

And out onto 33rd Street, daylight already gone, lights, the
noise and bustle, and Helena's arm up — such a strong arm —
hailing a cab. And then the drive up 8th Avenue, up, up, a word
or two with the cab driver: cold, isn't it? Left at the circle onto
Broadway, becoming Amsterdam. Left onto 79th, then right:
Riverside. Out, then, in front of my apartment, the cab door
slamming shut as the car pulled away, and Helena walking
towards our doorway, pulling her wheeled bag behind her.

An old building, seven storeys. Our doorman: oh, good evening, nice to see you! He knew her, of course.

I was more looking forward to Helena's visit than I thought.

ONE OF THE THINGS Helena and I did this visit was go and see the Tiffany mosaic of the two white swans at the Met. She knew it was a favourite of mine, she even remembered that Stephen's older daughter had loved it as a child.

We took a cab there, soft snow was falling as we drove, everything white. I would have seen more paintings and works and rooms, but a few were enough. We stood in front of the Tiffany mosaic.

It's called *Garden Landscape,* and it is a garden, with a serene, blue pool. Do you think it escapes me that it's a paradisal garden like ours in Johannesburg was? It doesn't escape me.

The mosaic: *tesserae,* and iridescent glass. If you look closely you can see each stone, each glinting stone a different colour, opalescent, with many, many blues.

Helena took photos of it with her phone that day. I don't think Mark's ever seen it, she said. It's wonderful. I nodded. It is, it is wonderful.

It's a summertime scene, a garden, as I said. With a pond, or stream of water, and two, white swans.

Afterwards Helena and I sat at the café alongside, tall windows overlooking the park, a vision in white with so much snow that day, and ordered tea, a carrot muffin for her, have something, Mom, she said. But I only had tea, a ginger tea. I felt very happy, then.

HELENA SLEPT in the room she had as a child, nothing has changed in it. Sometimes she says I should change it, perhaps it needs a coat of paint, Mom, she says. There's a painting of mine that occupies one wall, I only hung it there in recent years. It has many browns, many shades of brown, in it. Helena was so pleased when she saw it for the first time. Her bookcase is there, with some of her childhood books, although most of them she had taken with her, years ago, when she had her first apartment, her first job.

And I lent Helena Ta-Nehisi Coates's newest book, the one published last year. Actually, I said, take it with you, home, I've read it. You can have it. I pictured Helena's long train ride home, through the towns, the snow: Holyoke . . . Brattleboro . . . White River Junction . . . Randolph. She'd have a new book to read.

The book I first thought to lend Helena was *Snow Country*, I forget the writer's name, he's Japanese. It's a love story. To my mind it's a spare book, filled with many spaces, quiet spaces, not overfilled with words. Perhaps it's the translation from Japanese that gives this effect, but I don't know.

I thought then that Helena wouldn't like that book, so I didn't mention it. Its cover is a deep, clear blue.

Helena cooked for me again, this time I didn't protest, she was going to do it anyway. She cooked another soup, a vegetable soup, perhaps it was squash, it was so deep a colour. We ate, we sat over the steaming bowls, there was fresh, crusty bread Helena had bought. We sat talking afterwards in the soft light, the snowflakes falling outside, you could see them. We talked about Nicholas, about his plans. She said she missed Howard — her dad. She remembered him taking her swimming in the river in Villiers, she talked about that, about the river in Villiers. And I said: me, staying at the house and reading on my blanket! Was I a selfish mother, Helena? Oh Mom, she said, not at all.

But she had to say that, didn't she?

I suddenly remembered my own mother. She was so far away, in that cemetery near Villiers, and for a moment I felt dizzy to think of the distance that separated me from that cemetery: from my mother's tombstone, alongside my father's. I had never actually stood in that cemetery, it is not I who buried them.

And then Helena said, let's go to bed. We turned off the lamps, one by one, and the room darkened, by degrees. I left one lamp on, I leave it on at night, because I wake sometimes. The lamp shed its soft light in a circle, and we turned then from the room.

At my bedroom door Helena leaned towards me. I'm taller than her, and she embraced me, I could feel her firm, strong body against mine. Goodnight Mom, she said. And I told her I was glad she had come. I was.

We went to bed.

And I thought how I'd be alone again on Tuesday, in this apartment, so quiet. I have my books, I do read, I've said that.

But I thought then that perhaps Helena had reason to worry, to worry about me. I said nothing.

I VISITED ERIC'S STORE and told him I was feeling much better, perhaps something new was about to begin with my painting, I had felt its pulse again. Eric was so pleased. I think we need more than tea to toast this, he said. It's not time to toast yet, I said, I'll let you know when I've actually done something to the painting. And he laughed. How incremental our progress was with our work, how painfully slow. I was glad, again, that I could talk to Eric.

But Eric had some big news. Eric was going to study in London for a year, he had got into a course run at the Royal Academy. I was thrilled for Eric, but what would I do without my weekly visits to his shop, our tea, our commiserating about our work?

Visit André when I'm gone, he said, he's nice to talk to. I can't substitute you just like that, you know, I said. I know, I know, I'm just trying to help, he said. I'll miss you too.

Eric had a goodbye party, it was held at the gallery of a friend of his. Howard and I went. Eric's friends from art school were there, Eric's parents, and other friends of his I recognized from gallery openings. And André was there. Howard hadn't met André before, I was so happy to introduce them. André framed your painting, he frames all my paintings, I said to Howard. And Howard said, oh, Jacqueline's framer, such a pleasure to meet you! She's always talking about 'her framer,' she's at her framer, she's going to see her framer, she must ask her framer . . . you're almost as important to her as Eric is, he said, and laughed, and André laughed too. Tall, handsome André, a shock of dark hair falling across his forehead.

And then they had a long conversation about business: about André's business, then about Howard's business, and I drifted off to look at some of the paintings on the walls. They were political works — some of them quite direct, not symbolic, but slogans, that kind of thing. They were works by a new Black artist, and this was important, so important, how I understood that. We — we who spent time in galleries — understood that. The gallery owner took risks showing this kind of work, he risked the work being censored, even his gallery being shut down, at any time.

The artist himself was there, surrounded by people, raucous conversation, then more serious tones. I thought I should go up to him and meet him, talk to him, but I felt intimidated by the crowd around him, I stood for a few moments on its periphery, I'm sure I looked lost, and so I wandered off again, to look at the paintings.

It was a hot summer night, and the back door was open onto a patio where drinks were being served. I went out then and stood under the black, starred sky, and took a glass of white wine from the server, the glass so cool in my hand.

There were some children, Eric's nieces and nephews, darting about under tables and chairs and for a moment I wished I was them. And I thought briefly of Stephen and Helena, at home with Emily. Stephen eating a plate of Emily's stew in the kitchen, the stew he relished and ate only when we were out, and which I only knew about because Emily told me. Helena was probably already in bed. I could have brought them, I thought.

And then I thought: I should bring them to galleries more often.

I REMEMBERED TAKING Stephen once to the Johannesburg Art Gallery, the main art museum of the city, it was a sunny weekday, he must have been five or six years old. We walked up the stone stairs of the multi-pillared entrance, overlooking the park, Joubert Park. It should have been beautiful, but it was not. I felt no pride in that museum, there were old European artists, dark hallways, improperly lit, I felt it to be a place filled with irrelevant art, irrelevant to us, in South Africa. And it was, it was . . . irrelevant. Irrelevant to what was actually going on around us. Stephen must have felt my quietness, my subdued mood, as we wound slowly through the galleries, such a small boy!

I bought him an ice cream from the Black man selling from his cart outside, we sat on a bench as he ate it. I remember the ice cream dripping down his chin, melting, melting: a hot, sunny day.

I didn't take him there again.

Of course that changed in New York. The children's early years, their holidays, their weekends, were filled with visits to museums, to galleries, to art openings. But that was different, everything was different, here.

AND THEN, as I toyed with my glass of wine and stood alone in a corner of the patio, Eric came out. Jacqueline, he said, I was looking for you. I was telling André to look after you in my absence, I told him you drink tea without milk, we sit on high stools, at three o'clock on Wednesday afternoons . . . He was only half joking. I smiled, ruefully.

And I want you to meet my parents, he said.

My friend Jacqueline, Eric said. His parents were so proud of him, winning a scholarship to study overseas. Eric, I said, you didn't tell me a scholarship! I knew he'd got into his course, a competitive course, but he had been too modest to mention the scholarship. Or perhaps Eric understood my own stasis with my work — he did — and didn't want to make me feel worse. Eric, whose career was on its way.

And then, at the end of the evening, Howard and I said goodbye to Eric. I hugged him; I felt close to tears. Come back, I said. Come back when you're done. Oh I will, he said. I want to see your painting finished.

We drove home, a quiet drive through the streets. André knows quite a bit about some of the companies I work with, Howard said, but I wasn't paying attention, I remember looking out into the dark trees.

I WENT TO SEE JOSEPH. I had bought some peaches at the Greek grocer, they were cling peaches, like the ones in my parents' garden in Villiers. Not as good, as fresh as the ones from Villiers, or perhaps I imagined that. But I had seen them and brought a box home, Josias carrying it in from the car. Like grandma's, Helena said happily, she bit into one and the juice spilled down her shirt, we all ate them greedily. I, even I. Their colour, their dusky orange colour. The Free State sun, they must have come from there. I imagined, again: the orchard, the trees behind the washing line, the rounding, ripening fruit, laden.

I've seen all kinds of peaches here, but not that kind. Or perhaps I've seen them, but decided they weren't the same, they wouldn't taste the same, I wouldn't bother buying them. And I don't like peaches any more.

But the cling peaches we had then were in their cardboard box in the pantry, the children would take one when they wanted. Wash them, I'd say. I'm sure they didn't wash them. And Emily complained about peach juice on the children's shirts: she leaning over the suds and washing board, washing, washing their shirts.

I'd take some peaches to Joseph.

Where did I get this idea? I could easily have said, Emily, take Joseph peaches when you take him his food, and Emily would have done that.

But I didn't say that, I didn't do that.

And the next afternoon I stood on a chair and reached into a tall cupboard in the kitchen, and took out a bowl, an ordinary wooden fruit bowl. We had plenty of bowls. I don't know why I remembered the wooden one, that was the one I wanted. And I filled it with peaches.

I had washed the peaches, they were washed.

The peaches, in a still-life. A Cézanne, I've said it before.

But Cézanne's peaches weren't cling peaches. I see that now. Cézanne's peaches have a dark pink, a red, bloom. Our peaches did not. But this is only something I think about now.

And I carried the bowl down the grass, to Joseph's room.

I SEE IT: February, a hot, still day. Josias was sweeping, sweeping the pool, the leaves, lifting the leaves out, the debris that fell from the overhanging trees. The children still at school. The dogs not out, they must have been sleeping in the backyard, their bowls, the flies, alongside. And Emily on her afternoon break, in her room. Did Emily lie down on her high bed, her bed raised on the bricks I had seen and knew, her worn brown shoes alongside on the stone floor, her plump frame: resting at last?

I, my pale legs, my sandals. My cotton skirt and blouse. My hair, my dark hair, smoothed over my shoulder.

Carrying the bowl, the wooden bowl, my two hands, I feel now the smooth wood, the weight, the roundness of the bowl, the fruit, walking carefully down the grass, the small hill, and into the trees, into the trees, at last.

And under the trees, a hidden place. I had to put the bowl down on the step, to knock on the door.

And the soft sound of the knock, some birds, a faint rustle of leaves. That's all.

Joseph: there at once, in his doorway.

His white shirt. Of course, his white shirt. Or perhaps that's only as I remember it. Memory plays tricks. The white shirt was the one I liked best.

I've brought you some peaches, I said, as I bent down to pick up the bowl. I stood holding the bowl in front of me. I think he was astonished.

I can't eat all those peaches, he said, and he laughed softly, thank you so much.

And I thought: yes, how could he eat all those peaches, this is a bowl for a family, a bowl for a house-full of people. And then: Joseph would get sick if he ate too many of them, he probably hasn't eaten much fruit in a while. And then: why had I not told Emily to bring him fruit before? I had thought of the basics: bread; milk; eggs. Protein. Once I had told Emily to take apples. So many ridiculous thoughts like this passed through my mind, but then he took the bowl, that beautiful dark wood bowl, from me, and turned with it into the room.

Come in, he said. And I stepped in.

I haven't had cling peaches in a while, he said. Such a treat. A treat: such a strange word, from him.

And I said, they're from the Free State, you know. The Unfree State you mean, he said, and laughed. I said nothing.

The door was still open behind me, I felt the dappled trees, their greenness, their gentle rustling sound. I felt, suddenly, as though I was in a bower, I felt the trees and their greenness were themselves in the room with me, around me, in a soft embrace.

But nothing was different. His papers and books still covered his table, his floor. I looked at the painting, still leaning on the ledge where I had seen it last time.

They're from the same place as the painting. The peaches, said. Yes, he answered.

And then he looked at me, properly. They are. It's your ce, he said.

Our place, I said, and I regretted immediately saying that. t's all of our place, I said. All, all of us. And then I felt close to tears.

He had put the bowl of peaches on top of the small, low fridge, where else to put it?

Please sit down, Jacqueline, here, the chair is for you. There was only the one chair.

But instead of sitting down I said, how long is this going to go on for, Joseph, how long?

He had no hesitation. As long as necessary, Jacqueline, as long as necessary. I could say he looked grim, perhaps that would describe it, but I, I must have looked stricken. I felt stricken.

But will there be a victory, real victory, one day, Joseph, will there? I can't believe it, I can't believe it, I said, and then I was overcome. I thought I must leave, and I turned, turned towards the door, the open door behind me.

But he strode across the small room, he reached the door before me and closed it, and he turned and said, stay, stay Jacqueline. Please stay. We can talk, Jacqueline, I can tell you what I'm doing. I can tell you.

I sat down then, in his chair, that hard wooden chair. And he stood, he remained standing, what else could he do? He could sit on the bed, but he didn't sit on the bed. He could have sat on the floor, but he didn't sit on the floor. He remained standing. And he spoke, then.

He told me about weapons caches, about military training in Zambia, in Tanzania. About the centres of resistance overseas, in London, and in Dar es Salaam. Dar, they called it. He told me about industrial targets, and he said, again: guerrilla war. It was far past sabotage, now. They had made progress, there was progress, it wasn't all for nothing.

At that I said, I know, Joseph, I read the paper. I know. You don't know the half of it, he said. You don't know the half of it. And: this is meant to reassure you, that's why I'm telling you, he said.

He stopped then, and looked at me. But I can't say any more, he said. He looked exhausted.

And then he said: come and lie with me, Jacqueline. He said it so softly I barely heard it.

I stood up. I must go, I said. I walked to him, to where he stood. And then I embraced him, I drew myself to him. I leaned my face against his shoulder, against his shirt: I had so yearned to feel that shirt. He held me then. And we stood like that, just like that, in the still room, for . . . for how long? I don't know for how long, I don't know.

And then I pushed away, and turned to the door, and left.

Do you believe me?

Is chastity harder to believe, than the carnal?

Do you believe we weren't lovers, that afternoon?

WHEN HELENA AND I were looking at the Tiffany mosaic, at the two white swans, this weekend, Helena said: swans mate for life, you know. I was silent. Like you and dad, she said.

I had no answer. But I thought: adultery. How does that fit, how does that fit, into it all?

I SAID THE children were strong — perhaps stronger than me. Helena made progress with her ballet, and I'd started taking her to watch the ballet every season at the Civic Theatre, a grand building on a hill in Johannesburg that Helena thought was 'royal.' There were *Swan Lake, Giselle:* all the classics. We'd spend a Saturday afternoon together going to the ballet, I would drive us, and I'd buy her a box of Maltesers at the refreshment bar, and she'd sit in her dress and sandals, the bright red box on her lap, taking one, one, once in a while into her mouth. They melt, those Maltesers, so sweet, I knew them.

And the auditorium, crimson too, velvet seats, glinting lights. I also loved the ballet, the motions and music soothed me and transported me, away from our troubles, away from all ordinary things. I've watched *Swan Lake* countless times since then, and it never fails to bring tears to my eyes. Perhaps that's why I like Tiffany's swans.

It has occurred to me that if Howard and I are the pair of swans in Tiffany's garden, I am the black one. This, too, is the truth. Perhaps I said that the other day to Helena, or perhaps I never said it, and just thought it.

But Tiffany's garden has only white swans.

STEPHEN SEEMED OBLIVIOUS of the room at the end of our garden in Johannesburg, and oblivious of our tension. Perhaps he wasn't oblivious, but I never saw any sign of concern, even interest, from him. He was busy with his swimming, and he worked hard at school. He was like Howard.

But one night at our house in the dark hours, everything silent and still, I was woken by Helena crying. I hadn't been woken by a crying child since she was small, a toddler, and I woke right away, with a start. I thought she must be having a passing dream and waited a few moments, tense under my covers. But the crying carried on. And then she was screaming. Howard was awake now too.

I threw back the covers and ran down the dark passage, turning on the lights, to Helena's room. She was sitting up, her hair tousled with sleep, her face crumpled, she was crying and crying. What's the matter, what's the matter, I said. I gathered her up in my arms, she was almost too big for me to do that by then, as Howard stood at the foot of her bed, saying also, what happened, what happened. The crying continued, in ragged jags, and then Stephen came in, rubbing his eyes.

A nightmare, she said, when she was finally calmer and able to speak. A nightmare, Mom, she said. What was the nightmare about, honey, I said, what did you dream? I don't remember, she said, I don't remember.

Is it possible that she dreamed of the man in the garden room and didn't want to tell us, to tell us how afraid she was? I have thought of that, over the years. Was she protecting us, her parents, because she knew it was so important, the man in the garden room was so important, and she had to be strong? I don't know. And what does it matter, anymore?

But for many nights we were woken by Helena's cries, all three of us, and we hurried to her room, and stood around her bed, I hugging and holding her, as we calmed her. And she always said: I don't remember, I don't remember the dream.

And each time, as Howard and I tried later to get back to sleep in our own bed, I would say to Howard, it's the situation with Joseph, of course it is. And how many times did I beg you to have this thing ended, have Joseph moved? Howard lay silent in the bed beside me.

Helena had trouble after those nights getting up for school, and Emily was told that Helena was having nightmares and waking up at night. So Emily fussed over her in the mornings and made special breakfasts: crumpets and butter; chocolate milk. And Helena would then head off to school, while I worried, and worried.

And Stephen started calling his sister a crybaby, this would start in the afternoons at the pool, and I would have to intervene, I'd be interrupted in my reading on the deck-chair. I'd have to scold Stephen and comfort Helena, there, there, he's horrible . . . until, finally, he'd stop.

And then Howard said, perhaps Sidney should be called. Sidney's not a psychiatrist, I said, and you know I don't trust or like Sidney.

We didn't call Sidney.

I wonder how Howard got through those days. I imagined him in his office on Rissik Street: the piles of paper on his desk the work; the hush. Perhaps work helped him, perhaps it always did.

And then, as suddenly as Helena's nightmares had begun, they ended. One night we were not woken, and then the next, and the next after that. Helena slept soundly, as she always had before.

I had told my mother about the nightmares on the phone, but I just said, it's a phase, I suppose children go through phases. My mother said, what's wrong, has something happened. She called every day. I pictured her holding the black telephone receiver, the wood floor of her house, her cacti. And asking: Has she seen a doctor, Jacqueline?

My mother suggested she and my father visit. A visit was due, she said. I told her it was out of the question, we were painting the spare room, definitely painting it now. Perhaps my mother could hear a note of panic in my voice that was new. Perhaps she was just too tired to argue with me. She said, alright, they wouldn't come. But weren't we sorry not to get this season's peaches, they were particularly delicious, and what about the children, wouldn't they miss the visit? I said we would manage, manage it all.

And then I was able to tell her the nightmares had stopped.

My own nightmares, though, had my mother straying down into the garden, down to the garden room. I pictured it: her low heels, her pale patterned dress, her stockings, on a wavering path down the grass, past the pool where the children were splashing, down, down to the glade under the trees . . . to see the garden, she would say. What has Josias planted down there, you have so much space to plant some

lovely things. That's what I imagined her saying. And I imagined her looking at the two rooms, the two stone rooms, not
far from each other. Which was Jacqueline's studio, she would
wonder. And another wavering walk to the stone step, the
stone step of Joseph's door. A turn of the door knob, a push
of the door.

My mind was getting the better of me. My mother would
never have done that.

And then I thought of my studio. I'd hardly been there.

HELENA, I said last weekend, d'you remember the Maltesers? We were having breakfast at my white-sashed window, the window looking down onto the trees. Helena had made scrambled eggs, toast. Mom, you're not eating, she said. I sipped my coffee.

The Maltesers, she said. *Swan Lake?* Those afternoons were nice, she said. Perhaps next time I come to New York we'll get tickets for the ballet, what d'you think?

I felt she was humouring me, trying to cheer me up. I don't need cheering up. I don't really want to go to the ballet. Big expeditions, especially at night, tire me: the cabs, the lights, bundling up for the cold, standing for a long time, the inter-missions. I don't want any of that. Also, I've seen *Swan Lake* enough times, that's what I've decided. Perhaps there is a limit to how often you can see *Swan Lake*. I never used to think that, but now I do.

Helena, I said, do you remember the nightmares? In Johannesburg.

Why are you thinking about all that, Mom, she said. I don't remember, no.

As I said, I will never know, I will never know what Helena's nightmare was.

MY PAINTING LIVES IN ITS permanent home, it lives across the park. In the years after it was acquired I would visit it from time to time, they were visits of pride and joy. With Howard I would walk, I've said how much I walked, how I learned to enjoy walking, here. It might have been on a spring day, the buds coming out, Howard and I still bundled in jackets for the chill, but loosening and opening our jackets as we walked. We'd walk around the reservoir, spread under the sky, the familiar, winding walk, the iron rails. The runners, the dog-walkers, the children in prams. I'd have Howard's arm in mine.

We'd reach the traffic light at Fifth Avenue, then cross, and walk up to 92nd, and turn in then, to the stone building. Such an ornate building. Such a distance from my stone room, my studio at the end of my garden. I never failed to think of it, of the distance we had travelled from there.

And Howard and I would remark, again, on the irony, Howard sometimes mocking me. The Jewish Museum. How is it that I, a Jew who tried, tried not to be a Jew, have my painting there. But what makes up the identities of art in that museum, what identity do you have to claim? Yes, I am Jewish. Did I have to be Jewish? I am Jewish. Born of a Jewish mother. I have, finally, to accept that.

And the elevator, not a large museum, its entrance cramped, the elevator up to the second floor, and the permanent collection.

Sometimes they had moved it, moved my painting. To another room, another wall. I became alarmed when I didn't see it, when it wasn't where I was expecting it. And I'd walk then from room to room, scanning the walls, Howard behind me, until . . . until I saw it.

It was such a relief then, when I saw it. Its whiteness. Of course. Its simplicity. That luminosity; how had I done that?

Critics have admired the artist's technical mastery: the use of a monochromatic, white-based palette to create a canvas infused, paradoxically, with multiple hues and shades.

Howard and I would stand then, in silence, looking at the painting. Once I was standing next to a Japanese man, he took a photo of the painting with his phone.

Critics have interpreted the painting's simplicity and whiteness as suggesting a wish, or quest, for spiritual transcendence, or moral virtue.

But other critics suggest that the painting is a depiction of erasure, even death.

The artist herself has said she feels any work of art must be open to multiple, even conflicting, interpretations.

Howard and I would move on then, and look at other paintings, so many other paintings. There were Chagall's lithographs, and especially: his doves. Not swans, but doves! Of course, they are white, too.

And then, down the elevator, out of the arched entranceway, into the sunshine: the light of the avenue, but dappled, by the trees.

And Howard and I would walk, we had a favourite coffee shop, but it was far down, on 75th, and across to Lexington. Such a long walk, we talked about so many things as we walked.

We'd have coffee at the small table outside, in warmer weather. Or inside, cramped, when it was colder. On winter days the windows steamed, from the bustle and noise of people inside.

They made good coffee. Or perhaps it was lunchtime, and Howard would have a sandwich, I more coffee. Howard never pressed me to eat. Howard knew that for me to eat was something of an ordeal, an imbibing of things, of outside things, of currents, that I didn't want. That I don't want. Senseless, to your ears, I am sure.

And once we went to the museum, it was an ordinary Tuesday, Howard had retired and wasn't working by then, and we couldn't find the painting. We went again through the rooms, retracing our steps, looking for it, then walked in the opposite direction, through all the rooms, the galleries, looking and looking for the painting.

But we didn't see it.

I felt then ill. Perhaps I'd imagined its presence there, altogether. Perhaps, I thought, I'd never painted it.

And I instantly remembered my studio, my garden room, the desolation: the painting's stasis, then death, in there, those years. The years I couldn't bring it to life again. Joseph.

They rotate the collection, you know they rotate it, Howard said. I knew that, of course I knew that. You'll call the curator when you get home, Howard said.

But my day was spoiled. It was a fall day. We walked home without going for coffee, we walked through the golden, reddening leaves, leaves fallen, leaves everywhere, leaves rustling around us, and people, children, dogs, tourists with cameras were joyful, joyful in the leaves, but all I could think of was the white, the snow and ice: the winter that would follow.

And of course it was an ordinary thing. The curators rotate the collection, there were months, even years, when my painting wouldn't be on display. I'm sorry, Mrs. Kline, the curator said when we spoke on the phone, I could have let you know before.

Yes, she could have, Howard said. She should have. We were home at the table at our window, Howard had bought a sandwich on the walk home, on Columbus Avenue, and we sat, the golden leaves spread below us and across the street outside. The city, a low hum, invisible. And I, not eating at all.

AND LATER I IMAGINED the painting in its place of storage. I'd been in storage rooms, the vaults of museums, galleries. But this was different.

My painting would not be alone, it would be in a room with others, close to many others. And under covers, elaborate covers, wrapped and sealed, hidden away.

I was lying in my room, my room I loved, on my dark bed, as I imagined this. I, recumbent, like my painting.

And then I thought: but my painting will be stored vertically, that's how they store paintings, they store them vertically. And they don't cover them, the paint surface has to be untouched by anything.

194

For a moment I remembered my mother's house in Villiers, and the dark wardrobe of dresses, my dresses. In darkness too, closed-up, all those dresses, a-rustle, against one another.

But the idea, the image of the painting lying flat, had soothed me. I pictured the conservator with his white cotton gloves: the humidity control panel; the temperature panel; the exact, exact light. The painting at rest.

The conservator would take care of my painting.

I slept.

L AST NIGHT I dreamed I took Joseph to the museum to see my painting. We were old, in the dream. It was Joseph, this time, who had his arm in mine, not Howard. And then I woke up, weeping.

Joseph never saw the painting completed. Of course, how could he have?

ELENA CALLED AGAIN. Are you feeling stronger, Mom, she said. I wished she'd stop asking me, but I couldn't say that.

It's icy out, Helena said. She's taken to reading the weather forecast for Manhattan every day, because of me. Be careful, she said.

T HE PAINTING WAS on display again last year, Helena saw it. More recent commentary was on the wall, she photographed it with her phone and showed me.

Critics suggest that the painting is a depiction of white power or supremacy, an interpretation especially relevant in the present moment.

A white painting by a white artist. Sometimes I think that such a work should be retired from the world, to make room for . . . other works. For historically erased artists and works, that's how they describe it.

I don't think I'd mind.

But it's only on some days that I think that.

SINCE MY VISIT to Joseph I read the morning newspaper on my patio with renewed attention. Or obsession. Some days I wouldn't find any report, any report I was seeking. No explosion. Nothing. Is it strange to say I felt disappointment?

But then the next day there'd be something: a weapons cache found, in a shanty on some small street, off the main Reef road or the main road to Cape Town, or to the Free State, something.

Joseph's work was proceeding. Their work was proceeding.

And then I'd think of his dark head bent over his table, and the quiet there under the trees.

I went nowhere near my studio.

I missed Eric. Eric was my friend, but my weekly visits with him had ended. I got a letter from him in London, on a blue aerogram, in black-ink pen and his back-sloping script. I remember when it arrived, one quiet day, I with nothing, no painting, but reading the newspaper reports, my morning search through the paper for clues, my routine conversations with Emily about the grocery list, Josias sweeping, sweeping the pool under the trees.

I wouldn't visit Joseph, I'd decided that, but I felt the invisible thread that must connect us. I on the patio reading the paper, the reports, as I sat in the dappled sun; he not visible, but there, beyond the trees.

Joseph was working. He would be writing, his dark head bent over his pages; his small, stone room.

ERIC'S BLUE AEROGRAM ARRIVED. A new colour, a new kind of letter. I'd seldom received letters from overseas.

Eric wrote about his course; about his new friends; about London. He wasn't enjoying the winter, he wasn't used to it. I had to buy a coat, he said. He made small observations that made me laugh, with his sense of humour I knew so well.

I saw someone who looked like you on Camden High Street yesterday, he wrote. You followed me, right? And: d'you take milk in your tea yet??

And then he wrote: I love being in a free country. I went to a shop in Islington run by the ANC, there were books and books and pamphlets about Mandela we've never seen. I stood there and wept, he wrote. And then: Maybe I won't come back.

When I replied, on a blue aerogram I'd had to buy at the post office, I told him about the lack of progress with my painting, about my despair. But everything else was alright, I said. The children fine. Howard sends his regards, I wrote.

I wrote nothing in reply to his political comments, to his comments about the ANC and Mandela. There were too many things I wanted to say, and none of them seemed possible to say. I couldn't mention Joseph, so that left me with nothing.

Eric could probably feel my mood, the stasis of where I was, in my letter. And then I thought: I should try to sound more cheerful. But then: no, I can't do that, I don't like to pretend. And then: I wish I could have told Eric about Joseph, I wish I had.

Later I remember looking out over the pool, the garden, and thinking how disconnected everything was, and how alone I was. Howard was still preoccupied with his work, and I had stopped asking him about Jack Benator, it seemed we accepted it was safe to have Joseph with us, so he would just stay.

And then I thought of my mother. Perhaps this was how my mother felt every day, as she sat on her porch with her knitting, her bag with the tortoiseshell handle, next to her cacti. The blank street in front of her, only Maggie, Maggie who could be called — summoned — to come.

And what use was Maggie? I pictured her bleary eyes, the hot yard where she'd be sitting. On her chair, under the narrow shadow cast by the roof of the house.

But I was not my mother.

Joseph, I thought. Joseph.

Joseph held a different future for everything. What Joseph was planning would change everything, it would shift everything. No: overturn everything. Howard was not wrong to have Joseph with us; it was right, the right thing to do.

I went back into the house and felt much better. I called my mother. Mom, I said, you should do something different sometimes. What are you talking about, she said. Jacqueline? And then I felt very impatient and said I had to go.

I FORCED MYSELF to go into my studio. And then I'd sit for hours, my head against the chair back, my eyes closed. It was still a peaceful place. I fiddled with some acrylics, I had bought some from Eric's shop before he left. Try acrylic for a while, he said, maybe something will shift for you. I would try that.

And then I thought: the real problem with my painting started when Joseph came, when Joseph moved into that room. It disturbed me so much, his being there. It was as simple as that.

And that night I had a terrible dream. I woke, in the dream, in my bedroom, and got carefully dressed. I smoothed my hair, my hair so beautiful, in my mirror, in the dream. And then I went to my car and drove, drove . . . towards the city. In the dream the streets were empty, the grey streets, because everyone was at work, or at school, everyone, but me, me. And I drove past all the buildings, through the traffic lights, stop, go, stop, go, until I got to John Vorster Square, the central police building of Johannesburg, I knew it, it had many floors, it's a blue building, and I parked my car and got out, and then I glided, I was gliding, into the building. And I went up to the man in uniform at the desk and put my arms, my bare arms, on his desk. I'm here to report something, I said. And the man stood up as though he'd been expecting me, *mevrou,* he said, this way. And I followed him into a room, a grey room, and men, men in uniform said, *mevrou, mevrou,* and they bowed. The security police. And I sat, then, and I spoke. I told them about a man in my garden room, he was their man, they could get him, go and get him, any time. They must go and get him.

I heard my soft voice as I spoke.

And then I woke up, in horror.

Joseph.

And at eight o'clock in the morning I walked from the patio, my tea untouched, my newspaper unread, I walked straight down to Joseph's room. He wouldn't be there: he'd be gone, he'd been found. Or he'd been moved, without our knowing. I felt the way I remember feeling years later in New York, when Stephen, a teenager, came home late, later than he'd said, past midnight, and we waited up for him, certain he wasn't coming home, at all.

And I didn't knock, because I truly feared Joseph wasn't there. I opened the door and stood there.

A cup — tea? — was wreathing steam faintly on his table. Joseph sat, a pen in his hand. He looked up at me. In shock. I don't know.

And then I was against him, my head against his beard, he'd stood up, the chair was knocked over behind him. And we stood like that, for a long time, I clutching him as though my life depended on it.

And did I lie with him then, on that narrow bed?

I did not. I did not. And I told you I won't tell a lie.

I left from that chaste embrace and ran from the room, up the grass, past the pool, Josias sweeping, sweeping those leaves, and into the house.

MARIE, Stephen's wife, called yesterday. We have our subscription seats to the ballet, she said, will you join us, it's *La Sylphide*. It's next Thursday. I knew right away that this was Helena's plan, Helena who was worried, and wanted me to go to the ballet. A conspiracy, among them, to take care of me, to worry about me.

Oh Marie, I said, thank you, dear, I don't like going out at night, and in winter.

She tried to persuade me, she said they'd pick me up in the cab, travel with me to and from the Lincoln Center. You'll enjoy it, Jacqueline, she said.

She calls me Jacqueline, not mom.

How are the girls, I said. Fine, everyone's fine, she said. Let me know if you change your mind, we'd be delighted.

But I'm not going with them to *La Sylphide* next Thursday.

I READ IN THE PAPER: raid on weapons cache. Another one. Cache. *Cacher*. To hide.

I was hiding so much. I spoke to nobody.

I've said before: my children are strong. They went to school, Stephen did well and swam in his team. I drove Helena to her ballet classes, she progressed, and passed from one level to the next, practising her pirouettes around the dogs, who barked and barked.

Josias was quiet and did his work, or perhaps he didn't do that much work. I didn't watch, or care. Perhaps the pool had more debris and leaves floating on its surface than usual, I heard Stephen once complaining to Josias, hey, Josias, too many leaves in the pool, too dirty! Josias ignored him and smoked his cigarette on the chair near the dogs, as always.

Emily seemed preoccupied, she told me Albert was having trouble with the children in Alexandra, the children running, running in the dust behind the houses, and Albert's mother now living with them. But Albert's mother was old — her legs were bad — and she couldn't help much.

I told Emily I was coming down with something, I must rest.

Howard came home tired, tired lines around his eyes, I saw them now.

AND THEN I WROTE to Eric, on a blue aerogram. He'd sent me one of his letters, filled with funny and interesting things. I thought: I can't keep replying with gloomy letters, without explaining what's wrong.

I started my letter in the usual way, with news that was not news: painting stalled; children and Howard alright.

And then I wrote: Eric, there's a man I have to tell you about. Why, why did I write that?

But then, here's what I didn't write:

I didn't write: Eric, I want to sleep with him.

I didn't write: Eric, I've fallen in love with him.

I didn't write: Eric, should I sleep with this man?

Instead, I wrote: Eric, the resistance here is alive and well, you'll be happy to hear. A man working for the ANC is staying with us. He's working underground; a fugitive. He stays in the garden room right near my studio, at the end of my garden. Take courage, Eric.

And then: Yours, Jacqueline.

It felt like a triumph of sorts, to tell Eric that we here were working towards something, some kind of breakthrough, even though it didn't seem like it.

I thought then about letters being intercepted by the security police, that was happening. But why would the security police intercept a letter from me, a woman in the northern suburbs of Johannesburg, writing to her art student friend in London? They wouldn't intercept such a letter, they'd have no reason to intercept such a letter.

I took the blue aerogram, folded it, and sealed it. I put it on my mantel, and the next day I took it to the post office on Corlett Drive, and sent it to London.

I felt a lightness. I no longer had a secret, or I had one secret less. Eric, free and far away from everything, in London. I should have told him long ago.

THE NEXT MORNING I went to my studio and took out my canvas, my painting on its easel, and moved it into the best spot, the best light. And it had a clarity that morning, that I hadn't seen before. I thought of Eric: he would be so pleased. I would push on. I would finish the painting one day, after all.

I had days then of great happiness, it seemed to me. I paid more attention to the children, I was more generous to Howard, I asked him how work was, I was sorry he had so much work. I called my mother and told her about Helena's ballet progress. I told her about Stephen and his swim team. I even found myself joking with Josias in the kitchen, the kind of jousting with him that was Howard's way.

I listened sympathetically to Emily about her troubles in Alexandra, and suggested she take an extra day off the next week. She was very pleased.

And the morning newspaper: I looked with renewed excitement for the reports, because they were Joseph's work, such important work. Was it my imagination that incidents — explosions — in random towns, were becoming larger, and more serious? But I knew the clampdown would be harder, more serious too. I, though, I was stronger. It would be fine.

I thought of Eric as my distant, essential, friend. I waited for his next letter from London.

And I went to see Joseph. I took him a bar of special chocolate that Howard had brought from his office, a gift from a client. I think he was amazed, he opened it and broke a piece of chocolate off right away, and laughed. You're in a good mood, Jacqueline, he said. I am, I said. Perhaps everything will be alright, I said. I'm painting again, I said. Oh, that's wonderful, he said, and I felt he truly understood what that meant to me.

Come out and walk with me in the garden, I said, come on. He laughed. Are you crazy, he said. What's come over you, Jacqueline? How I wanted to walk with him in my garden, his arm in mine. To sit on the white bench that was well back, under the trees.

I'll walk freely one day, he said. Don't worry about me, I go out at night. Sunshine, sunshine, I said, in a playful, sing-song voice, you need sunshine. He shook his head. I wanted to put my hand against the side of his face, such a beautiful face. I would feel the bristle of his beard against my hand. How I feel it, as I'm talking to you now.

But I didn't do it. I left.

I told you I won't, I must not, tell a lie. I never slept with Joseph Weiss, I didn't do it.

No LETTER FROM Eric in London came. Two weeks, three weeks. It would turn to autumn soon. It was March 1973. Joseph had been with us for fourteen months.

I was sleeping well, long hours, through the night.

DURING THE SMALL HOURS, perhaps three o'clock in the morning, of March 26th, we were asleep in our house. A family, safe and dreaming: how I see us all in our soft white beds, hardly stirring, softly breathing. Emily and Josias, asleep too in their rooms, each of them, on their beds, those iron beds. The dogs asleep, sprawled and still, in the dark, stone yard.

And a noise woke me, that I knew at once came from the backyard. Dogs barking, but many dogs barking. Men's voices shouting, but many men's voices. Voices in Afrikaans. Emily — it sounded like Emily — shrieking. The sound of wood splintering and the sound of it again. Dogs again, hysterical. Emily's voice, hysterical. More shouting, swearing, and then the sound of thudding feet, of running. *Jou moer.* And then, after a brief lull: unmistakably, the same noise, but coming from the garden now, not the yard on the side of the house, near the gate, the dogs. For several minutes I listened in horror, Howard awake now too. More shouting in Afrikaans, *opstaan opstaan,* a dog yelping, it was in the garden. More minutes, long minutes. *Die fok van hier af.* Then, again running, and swearing. Thudding. Wood splintering. More running, then a brief lull, again. And finally from the road, car doors slamming, engines started, the dogs hysterical, still. And as I and Howard put on our dressing gowns and ran to the kitchen, to the yard, we saw the children — the children! — coming from their bedrooms, rubbing their eyes, too.

Emily was already on her way to us, she was at the kitchen door, Josias with no shirt on behind her.

They took Joseph, they took Joseph, Emily said, her breath came in jags. Her face shone with sweat under the yard light. Josias stood, speechless. And Howard.

It's Howard's face that I will always remember. A man disarmed. Shattered. And the children crying and crying, inconsolable.

WE WENT AT DAYBREAK to see Joseph's room, the sun rising as it always did, on a day that was different to any other before it. There was his splintered door, battered in. His chair and table, overturned. And everything, everything else apart from the bedsheets, gone. No paper. No book. No pen. No briefcase. Nothing. His small fridge still filled with ordinary things: milk, butter, cheese, a plate of leftover something. And his bathroom: a white towel hanging, a bar of soap in the shower. Nothing else.

I, Howard, Emily, and Josias stood in the room, as in a wreckage. The children had gone to sleep finally, exhausted, an hour earlier.

Howard, hands limp at his side, Josias silent, as though struck, and Emily lifting, lifting the bedsheets, the blanket, to see if something, something of Joseph remained.

The painting, the painting had been knocked off its ledge and lay on its face on the floor. Its brown paper back, its backboard, had been gashed and pulled out, torn out, revealing only the canvas below. It was not worthy of taking, of examining further.

IN THE DAYS THAT FOLLOWED there were the frantic questions. From Jack Benator: who had betrayed Joseph, who knew where he was? Howard counting, again and again, the people who knew about the garden room: the six of us. Me. Howard. Stephen and Helena. Emily. Josias.

Tiny? Ah, Tiny never cared what Joseph was doing there, not Tiny.

One of the children, did one of the children say something? Never, I knew that would not be.

And another mystery: why had the police not come for us, as well? Because we had found, that terrible morning, that the door to my studio had been battered, splintered open, too. Some of my frames tossed aside, things tossed aside in a search, but a cursory search. It seemed the police had quickly seen there was nothing that interested them, there.

And as the days wore on there was a slow dawning: the police had deliberately left us. They had come for Joseph, and decided not to come for Howard, or for me. Jack Benator too: untouched.

And then, one morning a few black days later, as I was saying goodbye to the children going to school, I remembered something. How had I not thought of it before?

Eric.

I WENT OVER the words in my last letter to Eric, in my mind. I went over them, again and again. And again. All I could hear in my head were my own words: *A man working for the ANC is staying with us. He stays in the garden room right near my studio, at the end of my garden.*

That's what I'd written. I had written it.

I said nothing to anyone, I said nothing to Howard. I told no one.

I, I alone, was responsible for what had happened.

I thought about dying. I felt like dying.

I BECAME, then, truly ill.

No one could talk to me. Howard stayed home from work, and sat at my bedside. Emily came back and forth with tea, meals for Howard. I ate and drank nothing. I don't know what the children did, how they managed, I think they went to school.

I imagined the interception of my letter, as I lay. My aerogram being opened by the security police, in a grey, grey room, in Johannesburg's central post office, I knew that building, an old, grey place. I pictured my black-inked words, read, again, and again, by cold eyes, as they swam in front of me, endlessly across my mind: my own black words.

And I imagined the quiet order given by a man in uniform, by telephone, the information passed.

But then lucidity came, and I thought of another possibility. A possibility even worse. Perhaps Eric had received my letter in London.

Eric's face entered my mind. It hovered, pale, with a small smile: a familiar face, become a nightmare.

Was Eric an agent of the government, an informer?

London, and the shop in Islington with books about Mandela that he'd written about in his letter? Perhaps that was Eric doing field work, research, for the government, finding what was out there, overseas. Was that it?

Was Eric sending information from London, helping to infiltrate and undermine the resistance?

I knew about such agents, I knew they were everywhere. Never, never, would I have dreamed Eric was one of them.

And leaving me and Howard out of it? Maybe that was

the worst of all.

Was that Eric's way of being a friend, was it?

I imagined it, Eric's communication with his superiors: *the owners of the house have nothing to do with it, they're harmless. Kline does big corporate work for you guys, he's not a political guy. Leave him out of it. The wife: harmless. She paints pictures. LEAVE HER OUT OF IT. LEAVE KLINE OUT OF IT.*

The wife: harmless. She paints pictures. LEAVE HER OUT OF IT.

That's what I imagined, as I lay.

SIDNEY WAS CALLED. He came and gave me sleeping pills, which I took, and I told you I've never taken a drug. I heard Sidney tell Howard a psychiatrist was needed, he could do nothing to help any more. Howard said nothing, he could say nothing about what had happened.

And then my parents arrived.

I don't know what Howard told them. Jacqueline is sick, that's all.

THE TRUTH AND RECONCILIATION COMMISSION which began in 1996 didn't discover who betrayed Joseph Weiss to the police in March 1973. It turns out that history doesn't record everything that happened, every last fact.

Howard, eighty-three years old when he died last year, never knew who betrayed Joseph. I never told him.

Helena doesn't know.

Only you know who betrayed Joseph to the security police, now.

Today helena called me and we had a long argument about *La Sylphide,* about Stephen and Marie. You'll enjoy it, Mom, why don't you go? They'll have the best seats. Come on, Mom, go. She sounded exasperated.

What I don't like is how she tells Stephen and Marie her worries, and then they start worrying. And then they ambush me with a plan. Is it not enough for me to say to Helena I don't want to go to the ballet, and have her leave it at that?

MANY WEEKS AFTER the March day of 1973 when Joseph was taken, I started to recover. I recovered enough to look after the children again, and to go through the semblance of an ordinary day.

Perhaps Sidney's pills helped me.

My parents in the spare room also helped. They knew and understood nothing of what had happened, but they could see something had happened. Perhaps my mother thought it was a problem between me and Howard, I don't know. Now and then she'd look at me and say, what happened, Jacqueline? This enraged me, and she quickly learned not to ask anything anymore.

But she planned meals with Emily in the kitchen, and sat on the patio under the trellis with her handwork, her knitting, in the afternoons. My father talked to the children, humoured them. He asked them about homework, or helped them with homework. I don't know.

Howard went back to work.

And one day I went down for the first time again to the garden room. It was as we'd last seen it, even the chair still overturned. Emily hadn't bothered to take and wash the bedsheets, the towel. The door broken and splintered on its hinges, gaping wide. A ransacked room.

The painting, its back slashed and gaping also, was still on the floor where we'd left it. I picked it up and turned it over. The canvas was still intact.

I took the painting then, and went to my own studio, next door. Another ransacked room. I'd not been in there either.

AND ONE MORNING, as I paged through the newspaper on my patio, I saw it:

Joseph Weiss, lawyer and anti-apartheid activist, working underground for the ANC and Umkhonto we Sizwe, was arrested in a dawn raid in the northern suburbs of Johannesburg. He faces charges under the Sabotage and Terrorism Acts. If convicted he faces twenty years to life in prison. He was remanded without bail and will remain in custody at John Vorster Square until trial.

My newspaper had managed to report this event. Weeks after it happened, it is true. But reported, at last.

That newspaper had many more years of battles ahead, but this was one small victory. If victory you can call it.

O N THE SUNDAY of Helena's visit last time, she brought out a box of photographs from the cupboard in her room. They were old, some yellowed. There was one of her and Stephen, standing at the edge of our pool, hand in hand, she in that green swimsuit we liked so much. There was a picture of Stephen holding a trophy, and photos of Chester and Teddy, of me and Howard. I on my pool-chair, reading a book, caught unaware by the camera. Happy pictures. Some were taken at the beach by the sea, with Howard's sunburned face. And there was one of my mother in Villiers, her rose garden behind her. She had a tentative smile, which was typical of her. Who had taken that photo?

And Helena said, I wish I could visit the cemetery in Villiers where they're buried. She's never said that before.

How often I've thought of that cemetery near Villiers. A small Jewish cemetery in the middle of the veld, far from everything. An iron gate, forlorn headstones with Hebrew lettering. Pale weeds, an endless sun.

And I said, well you know I've never visited there either. It was Uncle Bernie who buried them, remember?

I remember, Helena said.

WE CAME TO New York.
Jack Benator helped Howard with the arrangements, because Jack was planning emigration for himself and his family too. Visas; bar exam; bank accounts. Everything.

Slowly I had packed up my studio. Its broken door was never repaired. But I felt I had to put the room in order. And I had to salvage something, something from that room, from my work. It was a long labour, picking and dusting, and laying down in piles, and sorting. I felt like a scavenger on a beach, a deserted, lost beach where a great tsunami had passed. Several mornings were spent this way before I felt I was finished.

And Jack's wife Madeleine helped us find our apartment in New York when we arrived a few weeks after they did. It is she who told us about schools, who helped set the children up at school. Madeleine Benator rescued me in New York.

MY PARENTS WERE SHOCKED that we were leaving. Why so suddenly, my mother said. But she had learned not to ask.

Howard is very unhappy with the political situation, Mom, we just don't want to live here anymore. I hear myself saying that, even now, and I remember my mother's astounded face as she heard me.

We told my parents they would come and visit us, in New York, imagine that! But no one could muster excitement for that, or even an image, of how that would be.

I recently imagined them, the two of them, in a small hotel we would have found them on West End Avenue, around the corner. My mother's pale dresses, her stockings, her handbags would have looked strange here, but perhaps in 1973 they wouldn't have. This is what happens when you impose an old, frozen image of someone on a new, different place.

We would have taken them to a Broadway musical, how I can imagine my father's face lit by the stage lights, entranced by a magical scene framed by the crimson-and-gold proscenium arch. He would have been seated next to my mother in the middle of the third row, because Howard would have got them only the best seats.

They would have been amazed to look out of our apartment window and glimpse the Hudson River through the trees, as Stephen or Helena, diligent schoolchildren, explained that following the river south just a few miles would lead you to the Statue of Liberty, and then, right then, the sea. And across that sea . . . a long way . . . was where they, where we, had come from. And millions of others besides.

My parents would have loved and been astonished by everything they saw.

But they never did visit us. They seemed to decline rapidly after we left, and to become old, at once. I was their only child, remember.

My uncle Bernard is the one who buried them, one after the other, and I remember again and again those phone calls with Bernard, and with his wife Elaine, the wire so crackly in those days, voices indistinct, as they spoke to us and let us know what was happening. *It's alright, Jacqueline, the doctor said there was no pain. No pain, Jacqueline.*

I never went back to Villiers, or Johannesburg, I've never been back. Another failure, a great failure, of mine.

On the other hand, I feel I am in that cemetery near Villiers, its pale weeds, its dry yellow grass, its iron gate, every day. And perhaps they lie, my mother and father, in peace there, after all.

I DIDN'T GO and say goodbye to André. He was Eric's friend, and I couldn't bear to hear or talk about Eric. And I was afraid. Perhaps André too was an informer, a government informer. I don't know, and I will never know, now.

Eric? I seldom say his name, I cannot. I got no letter from him, ever again, so I believe he betrayed us: me; the cause; everything. I have believed it all these years, and I believe it as I am telling you now.

I went to Howard's office one morning to say goodbye to Candace and Frederick Jones. Candace cried, she said she'd miss Howard. She'd not yet organized her art lessons, but she told me she would. Did she, in the end? I don't know, I don't know what happened to Candace.

Frederick Jones stayed on alone at the firm, he continued his corporate law practice for years after, Howard and Jack Benator were in touch with him sporadically. He was a good man — a good lawyer and a good man, both.

AND THEN came the day we said goodbye to Emily and Josias.

We'd sold our house. Our neighbours would adopt Chester and Teddy as their own. Helena and Stephen had said good-bye to the two of them, and in that moment it seemed to me this hurt them more than anything. I remember Helena's face buried in Chester's golden fur, and her crying and crying.

We were standing in our driveway, surrounded by a mound of bags and suitcases, it was August 15th, 1973. A cool day, in

Johannesburg. I remember the children in sweaters, Stephen's one my mother had made. (How I remember the blues in that sweater!) A taxi was coming for us. A flight to Rio de Janeiro (Mom, why can't we stop and visit there, I remember Stephen saying. It's just a stop, a two-hour stop, I said), and then one to New York. Such a long journey.

We'd never been to New York. Only Howard had, he'd been twice to arrange things in the last few months. The Benators were going to meet us at the airport, at JFK, the Benators who had recently arrived there themselves.

At first everyone had been happy and excited, Josias carrying some of the bags, Emily helping, Howard jousting with everyone. Who will carry your bags in New York, Josias joked, as everyone laughed. And the cooking, ma'am! (Emily said.) More laughing. Even I, laughing then.

And then: goodbye Emily. I went to Emily and hugged her. I'd never hugged her before. And then I couldn't let her go. Emily crying and mopping her eyes with her apron, and I crying, while Josias looked . . . stunned. And then the children started crying, both of them, again. And Howard was . . . I don't remember what Howard was doing. We stood like that, a strange family under the cool winter sun, our bags in piles around us.

And then the taxi came. It was a black car, I remember it.

WE HAD FOUND Emily and Josias jobs in the neighbourhood before we left, but it was rushed, and I don't know how suitable the jobs were for them, and I don't remember how the jobs turned out. And here is my other great failure: I didn't write to Emily and Josias more than once or twice. Perhaps I was overwhelmed by what faced us in our new home (I was), but that's an excuse. A year after we left, I had lost touch with them both, and I've never been in touch with them since.

Helena has asked me about that, a few times over the years. Could you Google and find them, Mom, she has said. I did Google Emily's name once, but found nothing. I found people with similar names, or people with her name, who couldn't have been her. I've told Helena that has been a terrible failure, yet another one, of mine. Perhaps Helena forgives me.

But here's a thing: I think Helena plans to visit South Africa one day. She doesn't say so, perhaps she thinks she'll alarm me, or upset me. Even last month, as we sat in my living room, just the two of us under the soft lamplight, she said, I was trying to Google Emily's name, Mom. Just tell me again: how exactly is her last name spelled? And I became irritated at once and said, there's no point, Helena, it's long ago.

But then she said: Emily lives in a free country now. And I couldn't answer her, except I said yes, she does. She does.

I told you: Helena is interested in all that.

JOSEPH WAS CONVICTED on all charges at his trial in December of 1973. We'd been in New York four months. How I remember the snow falling that day when Jack Benator told us, how we watched it fall and fall so softly, muffling and covering everything, every car and every lamplight, the tree weighed down with white outside our window. In that moment I felt that we'd be buried by all that snow for always. Perhaps I could not, did not, go out at all that day, perhaps that is true.

I THINK something in Howard was broken by what happened to Joseph. He wouldn't speak of it.

And he had to build his career again from the beginning, he had to earn a living and support us. The children, and I, needed him to be strong. He was.

IT WAS A LONG TIME before I started painting again.

Howard found the space on Columbus and rented it for me to use as a studio. He insisted on it, although I protested, telling him I no longer wanted to paint, at all.

And then all my canvases and paints and equipment that had been in storage were delivered there, to that studio, for me to start working, once more.

And, very slowly, I did. With the children settled in their new schools and getting older, I'd walk to my studio every morning, that lovely walk, in all seasons. Out the door of our building, its old tile floor, into the sunshine, good morning to our doorman in his grey-and-maroon suit, starting his job for the day. He, bantering with the colleague he'd relieved from night duty, the two of them talking and laughing, in

Spanish. Have a good day, madam! In spring, the leaves young on the tall trees along the river, so graceful, but no, not to the river, instead turning left on 84th, a dip in the street at West End, and then crossing Broadway: bustling babies in strollers, women with grocery bags, the man and his fruit stand (four bananas, one dollar), the other man, the old one, setting up his bookstand, a brief siren's wail, a man with bucket and soapy water and brush washing his pavement in front of the old hair salon, the Korean nail studio, I would see the girls lined up at their tables, customers already (so early!), and then turning right onto Columbus, and soon, my low shadowed doorway, the iron door, pushed. In the hallway, then, of my studio's building.

I told you I became a walker here. I forgot to say: I'd stop for my coffee at the shop a few doors away, and then go up, up the stairs (not the elevator!), to my studio — to my space.

I worked on many small canvases over the years, you've seen them. Perhaps I was healing. They weren't my best work, but they were work. I was creating.

I used only oil. I liked its longer drying time, the slow drying allows for manipulation, and minuscule changes, over time. I'd spend weeks and weeks on one canvas, first underpainting, then layering. Turpentine with a rag to thin and refine. Then re-layering. Days into weeks, drying. The mixing with my palette knife. And layering again. And again. Sometimes glazing between the layers, which added more time yet.

I was adding, adding paint, adding layers; a slow accretion of layers. Then I was taking away. And the taking away matters as much as the adding, you know.

I LEARNED TO COOK for the children, for Howard. Simple things: chicken, salad, vegetables. I'd buy groceries on my way home from the studio, and make dinner for everyone when they came home. And evenings Howard sat with Stephen and his homework, I see them still, their heads bent together under the lamplight, at Howard's desk.

We had found ballet classes for Helena, or should I say, Madeleine Benator found the ballet classes, and Helena thrived again.

I never took my painting, my large painting, out from its covers though. I just couldn't. I felt I couldn't.

AND EARLY ONE MORNING in 1985 Howard came into our bedroom with the newspaper, he'd been reading it with his coffee before he set off for work. Jacqueline, he said. He sat down on the bed. Read here, he said.

And I read:

Joseph Hyman Weiss, anti-apartheid activist and lawyer, member of the ANC and its military wing, Umkhonto we Sizwe, and colleague of Nelson Mandela, died in Pretoria Central Prison in South Africa on September 17, after a short illness. He was forty-three years old. He had been in prison since December 1973, convicted of charges under South Africa's Sabotage and Terrorism Acts. Full obituary to follow.

And I held Howard, he held me, we cried and cried, and were inconsolable there, on our bed, my rumpled sheets, in the dimness of our bedroom, for a long time.

I WAS OUT WALKING TODAY, and as I turned the corner onto my street, I caught a reflection in a glass window. I saw there an old woman, slight, in a dark coat. Her hair was smooth against her head, and snow-white. And then there were the dark hollows of her eyes. I stopped, and looked. You could mistake her for someone else, for some other old woman.

But it was me. It was, unmistakably, me. Reflected in the glass. It is me. Everything that happened, everything I did, everything I've told you, is me. All of it.

And I am old, now.

I HAD STARTED AGAIN on my large painting only when I saw freedom was actually coming, it was going to come, to South Africa. That was around 1990. I didn't plan it that way, but I felt a freedom within myself, a loosening, slowly, so slowly.

I started to work on my painting, and then . . . I finished my painting. That's the story, really. That's all it is. And it's only a painting after all, it's not a life.

It's not a human being's life.

On the other hand, perhaps I made, in my painting, something good, that is also incorruptible. Because outside of a painting, anything is corruptible. You know that.

A ND PERHAPS you've wondered about something else?
     In my bedroom, next to the dresser where only I see
it, is a painting. It's the painting I gave Joseph for his room.
I rescued it from there, long ago.

The painting . . . is the Vaal River. Nobody knows it's the
Vaal River, because it's an abstract. But I know it's the Vaal
River. And it's Joseph's painting.

I look at it every day.

ACKNOWLEDGEMENTS

I thank Deborah Willis, Kelsey Attard, and Freehand Books, for embracing this book, editing it, and bringing it into the world with such skill and care. I thank Antanas Sileika, Karen Smythe, Terry Grogan, Leslie Shimotakahara, and Diana Fitzgerald Bryden, for insight, help, and friendship; and Kathryn Kuitenbrouwer and Chester, for time to write in the beautiful space. I thank the Ontario Arts Council. And I thank my husband and two children, for their belief in this book from the beginning.

A NOTE ON THE TYPE

This book was typeset in Prospectus, designed by Dave Bailey.
It's paired with Sweet Sans, designed by Mark van Bronkhorst.

DAWN PROMISLOW was born and raised in Johannesburg, South Africa, and has lived in Toronto since 1987. Her collection *Jewels and Other Stories* was long-listed for the Frank O'Connor International Short Story Award, and named one of the eight best fiction debuts of 2011 by *The Globe and Mail*. *Wan* is her first novel.